Zombies Can't Swim
And Other Tales
Of The Undead

Other Books by Colin M. Drysdale

For Those In Peril On The Sea

Preface

When I started seriously writing *For Those In Peril On The Sea*, I really wasn't too sure if it would ever see the light of day. Now, almost two years later, it has been published to much acclaim, and I find myself not only halfway through the sequel, but also with a growing collection of short stories. In these short stories I've explored a variety of different zombie- and post-apocalyptic-related themes which wouldn't fit neatly into the three (or possibly four) books I'm planning to write in the *For Those In Peril* series.

Some of these, such as *The Girl At Little Harbour*, provide additional backstory for specific events in *For Those In Peril On The Sea*, while others, such as *The Wall*, are little offshoots of the main themes that I wanted to explore within my novels. Then, there are the more traditional zombie stories, such as *When Death Came To Flannan Isle*, into which I've introduced a twist here and there.

There are also stories I've written to explore different forms of writing, such as flash fiction (e.g. *The Bookshop*), micro-fiction (e.g. *Nightwatch*) and even a story that's so short that, excluding the title, it will fit in a single posting on Twitter.com (*The Watcher*).

Finally, there's a story called *When The Comet Came*, which, while it doesn't contain zombies, is still about the world coming to an end, and fits within the general post-apocalyptic genre, in which I seem to have been writing frenetically for the last couple of years, and of which I, myself, am a big fan.

While these stories are set in a variety of locations around the world, several of them have a particularly Scottish twist. This is, in part, because I'm setting the sequel to *For Those In Peril On The Sea* in Scotland, but it's also because Scotland provides the perfect backdrop for zombie stories that stay well clear of the traditional, and some would say overused, 'escape-from-the-city' plotline found in zombie fiction (although I do stray into that territory in stories such as *Family*).

Lighthouses feature with surprising regularity in these stories, but then again, lighthouses are an important feature of coastal Scotland, particularly the west coast where I spent a lot of time in my youth. Of these 'lighthouse' stories, my favourite is probably *The Black Heart Of The Sea*. As a child, I came across a book called *Prevailing Spirits,* which contained a series of ghost stories which melded the Scottish traditions of storytelling and folklore with modern life. Ever since I read those stories (particularly one called *Holiday*), I wanted to write a short story in a similar vein. Finally, some thirty years later, I feel I've finally achieved this.

Almost all these stories were published originally on my blog and have been freely available as .pdfs on the website I put together to accompany *For Those In Peril On The Sea*. The idea of bringing them all together in a single volume came about after I wrote a particular story (*Zombies Can't Swim*), which seemed to provide the start of a perfect title for an anthology of these stories. I also figured that some people out there might appreciate having all these stories in one place, rather than having to look through numerous different files. However, to give some added value to this volume, there is one full-length short story, *The Black Heart Of The Sea*, which is not, and never will be, available elsewhere.

For most of the stories, I've added some additional information either about where the idea for the story came from, or any particular unique or interesting features about, it in an 'Author's Note' section at the end. I've also taken the opportunity to copy-edit the stories once again, and clean up any issues I'd failed to spot the first time round. On this front, I'd like to thank Sarah both for helping with editing this volume and for putting up with my constant hassling for her to give me her thoughts on story ideas and early drafts. If the zombie apocalypse ever comes, she knows I'll always be there to protect her!

As well as being posted on my blog (*cmdrysdale.wordpress.com*) and my website (*www.forthoseinperil.net*), some of these stories have also appeared elsewhere:

1. *Leaving* was published originally on the *Zombie Authors Blog* (http://zombie-authors. blogspot.co.uk/).
2. *Last Flight Out* and *The Wall* have appeared previously on the *Home Page of the Dead* Free Fiction section (http://fiction.homepageofthedead.com/).
3. *When Death Came To Flannan Isle* was included in *Zombies?! Zombies!!: An Anthology* (iUniverse).

4. *The Bookshop* was included in the *Feast of the Dead: Hors D'oeuvres* (Source Point Press), where the remit was to write short zombie stories without using the z-word.

Table of Contents

Page

*These stories are set in the world of the novel *For those in Peril on the Sea* by Colin M. Drysdale.

The Bookshop

I don't feel hungry anymore; I haven't since yesterday morning. I guess after a while your body just gives up expecting food. It must be different with water though, because my thirst keeps getting worse. I need to do something about it or it'll drive me mad, but it would mean going outside. Mark did that the day before yesterday and he didn't make it more than a few feet. I'd rather die in here than go outside and face them. But god I need something: beer, wine, Coke, anything. Hell, I'd probably even take a Pepsi. This thought makes me laugh. The old world's gone, yet the advertisers still have their hooks in me.

There's a half-hearted bang on the security shutter. They know I'm in here, but they also seem to sense I'm close to death because they're losing interest. At first, when I was still strong, they hammered on it almost constantly, and I was sure they were going to break through. Mark was still here then, so maybe that had something to do with it. We'd worked together in our tiny bookshop for six years, and while we'd never had many customers, enough came through the door to keep us afloat ... just. At first, we thought we'd got lucky, getting the shutter down in time to stop any of them getting in, but after a few hours, we realised we should have run the moment they first appeared. Instead, we'd locked ourselves in and were now trapped in a room filled with nothing but books. And they wouldn't help us survive. I know,

1

because I tried eating a couple of pages from *The Raven* on the third day, to see if it would ease my hunger. It didn't; it just made my stomach hurt. That's when Mark got the idea of making a break for it into his head. I did my best to talk him out of it, but his mind was set. So, as quietly as possible, we'd inched the shutter up, just enough for him to slide underneath, before I slammed it down again … and that was the end of Mark.

***

I've been sitting with my back against the counter for almost a day now; too weak to move. I wonder how many others there are like me: trapped and dying while *they* roam the streets outside. How many, like Mark, tried to run? How many have been killed? I'm guessing all of them. Yesterday, when I could still stand, I peeked through the little gap in the shutter. I found if I moved my head around I could see most of the street. I could see the pieces of Mark's body strewn across the pavement. Much of his flesh was gone, either torn off as he'd been killed or chewed off when they fed on him afterwards. I saw two of *them* too, crouched down, picking away at his skull. One poked at it with a bony finger, causing Mark's left eye to pop from its socket. It dangled there for a moment, swinging back and forth, before it was bitten off and swallowed.

A thought occurred to me: it mightn't have been painless, but at least Mark's death was quick. If I was braver I'd pull up the shutter and take my chances with *them*, rather than just sitting here,

2

doing nothing other than dying. But I'm not; I never have been. All I can do is wait for death to come, and wonder how long it will be before I'm finally free.

***

Author's Note: This story was written originally for an online horror magazine which went bust before I could submit it. The word limit for submissions was 600 words, and this comes in at 598. It's probably my favourite of the flash-fiction stories included in this book. Technically, you, as the reader, don't know for sure that the creatures outside are zombies, but this only adds to the tension. The specific issue I wished to explore with this is one which also crops up in a range of forms in other stories in this volume: that is, were a zombie apocalypse ever to happen, many people would end up trapped in whatever building they were unlucky enough to find themselves in when it happened. In some cases, they would be lucky and it would provide the perfect place to ride out the apocalypse, but for many they would simply become trapped in a place which was highly unsuitable for long-term, or even short-term, survival. As a result, they would face a range of difficult decisions. In the case of *The Bookshop*, it's the difficult choice between staying inside and starving to death, or going outside and risk being killed by the creatures that lurk there. Neither is a good option, but because of a snap decision made at the start of the zombie outbreak — to close the shutters and sit tight — these are now the only ones available.

I'm With The Band

'You know I was in a band before all this happened. God, it seems like such a long time ago, almost a different lifetime. We weren't exactly world-famous but we had our fans, and we did pretty well in our home town. We were playing the night it all kicked off. We were actually on stage. It was the largest gig we'd ever done, in an old cinema which had been converted into a club. It had this massive glitter ball in the middle of the roof, and I mean *massive*. It must have been like three feet across, maybe four; supposed to be the biggest in Europe or the country or something like that. Anyway, we were up there on stage just finishing off our set. We were doing our signature piece, a real anthem which always brought the house down. I was knocking out this mad rhythm on the bass, while Baz was doing his thing on the drums. Mickey was noodling away on his guitar, while Leon had both hands on the microphone; he was leaning on it, nodding along. Leon wasn't his real name, that was Donald, but he didn't think it was the right name for a rock star so he changed it. He chose Leon, after Trotsky, because he thought it was all left-wing and right-on. He didn't really know anything about politics though; he was just doing what he thought was cool.

'Anyway, everyone seemed to be really getting into the music, jumping up and down, moshing along, but then something changed. At first, it was hard to put a finger on it, just a slight shift in the energy in the room. I looked across at Mickey and saw he'd noticed it too. He shrugged and tipped his head towards Leon. He was still nodding along at the mike, trying to stay cool, but I could see by the tightness in his shoulders he'd noticed the change in the atmosphere too. Baz, as usual, hadn't noticed a thing. When he got really into it, I swear you could've set a bomb off right in front of him and he wouldn't have missed a beat.

'Then I noticed people weren't really paying attention to us anymore. Instead, they were looking round, showing each other their phones. I'd got used to people having phones at gigs over the last few years, holding them up in the same way people used to hold up cigarette lighters, or filming us as we played, but I'd never seen this before. I felt my own phone go off in my pocket, but I just ignored it, letting it go straight to voicemail. It rang off just as we came to the climactic ending of the song. It was this great crescendo, with Baz and Mickey and me all giving it laldy,[1] while Leon faced us, arms held out, mike in hand, head thrown back. We ended, expecting the usual rapturous applause, but instead all we could hear was people talking. I could tell from the look on his face that Leon was really pissed off at this reaction. He always was a bit of a diva — but then what lead singer isn't? — and I'd seen him lose it with audiences before. I glanced across at Mickey, wondering if we should do something to intervene, but he wasn't paying attention. Instead, he had his

---

[1] 'Laldy' is a great Scottish word which, if you're not familiar with it, means to do something with great vigour and vitality.

phone out and was staring at it with a confused look on his face.

'As I stepped towards Leon, he turned and faced the audience, his face like thunder and just started yelling at them: saying how disrespectful they were being; that we deserved better. That was when my phone went off again; this time, telling me I had a text message. I looked around. Baz was sitting behind his drums, arms crossed, watching Leon with this amused look on his face, while Mickey, unbelievably, was now speaking to someone on his phone. That's when I realised there must be something big going on, so I pulled out my phone and opened the message I'd just got. It was from my mum and all it said was that my dad was at the front door, trying to get in, and that I should come home as soon as possible. This really confused me because we'd buried my dad the week before. I was just about to call home to find out what was going on when I noticed a movement at the back of the room. Two bouncers rushed through the double doors, and were trying desperately to pull them shut, yet they couldn't because of all these people trying to get in. All around the room, I could see other security guys speaking frantically into their radios and running towards the doors, but before they could get there, they flew open and newcomers started pouring in. Except they didn't really look normal: they were all, like, beaten-up and disfigured.

'I glanced round at my bandmates, but none of them seemed to have noticed these new arrivals. Mickey was still talking urgently into his phone, while Baz was pissing himself laughing as he watched

Leon. Leon was getting more and more angry as the crowd continued to ignore him, and was now in full rant mode: screaming and swearing at them; threatening to jump off the stage and take them on, all of them, all at once. Meanwhile, the odd-looking newcomers were surging through the audience. At first, I thought they were just pushing them out of the way, then with horror, I realised they were attacking them, biting them, tearing at their clothes and their flesh. People were trying to fight back, but they were outnumbered as more and more of these dishevelled, dirty people streamed into the room.

'All I could do was stand there and watch in disbelief as this carnage unfolded in front of me. There was blood and guts spilling everywhere as people fought for their lives, all surreally lit by the spotlights glancing off the giant glitter ball which hung above them.

'Then the first of them, a woman, made it to the stage and started to drag herself onto it. Still, it seemed I was the only one in the band who'd noticed what was going on in the audience. I stared at the woman: her hair was lank and streaked with dirt, her skin grey and sallow, and it was clear she wasn't alive. There was no life in her eyes, instead there were just these dark holes which seemed incapable of seeing anything. Yet she knew we were there, or at least she knew Leon was. Reaching forward, she grabbed his left ankle and started pulling him towards the end of the stage. Leon finally stopped ranting and looked down. One glance at the woman holding his leg, and Leon recoiled in disgust and fear. Only her grip was firm and he'd managed to get the microphone lead wrapped around his body while he'd been yelling abuse at the audience. As he fell, another of the newcomers, this time a man, grabbed him and together the two of them pulled Leon, struggling and screaming, off the stage and into the audience. That was when Baz finally noticed something was wrong. There were more and more of these dead people pulling themselves onto the stage, and before I could even shout a warning, they'd surrounded Mickey and were biting and tearing at him.

As the first one approached me, I pulled off my bass and, grabbing the neck, I swung it as hard as I could. I felt it make contact, crushing the skull of this old man, who was staggering towards me, half his face already missing. Behind me, I could hear Baz trying to make a run for it, but he must have tripped over his hi-hat because I heard it crashing to the floor. This seemed to attract the dead people away from me and towards him. For a moment, I thought about trying to help him, but looking around, I realised that if I was going to get out alive, I'd need to leave there and then. I heard the sounds of the dead people crashing through the drum kit and Baz shouting as he tried to fight them off, but there was nothing I could do for him. Still clutching my bass, I fled off-stage and towards the back door. Behind me, I could hear the sound of the dead chasing after me.

'I know I should have done more to help the others, but the way I see it, if I'd done anything differently, I'd have ended up dead too. I still think about them sometimes, but most of the time I try not to. I think it's the only way I can cope: trying not to think about how the world used to be; trying not to dwell on the past. Instead, I try to focus on keeping myself alive and fighting the dead, as we try to take back the land which once was ours.

'There's no music in the world any more, no one has time for it. Instead, there's just the sound of battle, of destruction, and of death. That's why I'm in here drinking when I should be trying to get some rest before I head back to the front line. So, here's to how the world used to be. May it be like that again someday.'

***

Author's Note: The idea for this story struck me when I was at one of my favourite music venues (*The ABC* on Sauchiehall Street, in my home town of Glasgow, which really is home to the largest glitter ball in Europe!). Mobile phones have become an almost universal (and very annoying) feature of modern music gigs, with some people seeming to spend their entire time watching the band they came to see through a tiny screen, rather than watching them on stage.

This got me thinking about what would happen if something truly life-changing were to happen during a gig. In the old days, you'd have to wait until you got home and turned on the television, or maybe even until the next day, when you read a newspaper. Now, it is likely you'd find out about it instantly, because someone would phone or text you, to let you know what was going on. With a big enough event, such as a zombie apocalypse, it's likely that the entire gig could be disrupted by all the phones going off; much, I would imagine, to the dismay of the band. This then, was the jumping-off point for this story.

Zombies Can't Swim

The first time I saw the sign at the entrance to the boatyard I laughed so hard I almost crashed my car, but once I regained my composure I figured it was nothing more than a great bit of advertising. Now, as I smash through the gates in a stolen SUV, I wonder if the old man who ran it had somehow foreseen what was going to happen. Right now, it matter if he d or not, only whether he was right. I shot past the sign with its faded black letters standing proud against a once-white background, that's now a dull, dishwater grey, proclaiming its message to the world: *Zombies can't swim: Buy a Boat!*. I glance nervously in my rear-view mirror to make sure I'm not being followed: zombies might not be able to swim but they sure as hell can run.

***

When the zombie apocalypse came it didn't happen in the way it was portrayed in the movies. Rather than the dead rising from their graves, it was, instead, caused by a virus which infected the living, stripping them of everything that made them human and leaving a body ruled by one single urge: to infect others. That in itself wasn't a problem, rather it was the way they spread the virus: not through coughs and sneezes, but by the infected attacking and biting others. If this reminds you of rabies that's because it was rabies, only it had mutated. It no longer killed; instead, it just

11

drove people mad, whipping them into a frenzy where they'd attack anyone who was near. It also acted much faster than rabies used to, taking over infected people's brains in hours or minutes, rather than weeks or months.

It had built slowly, almost without anyone really noticing, starting with just a few cases in Haiti, but with everything else going on there it was hardly surprising that no one picked up on what was happening until it was too late. After all, at first, it was hard to tell the difference between attacks by those infected with the virus and the violent protests which had sprung up across the country, against the US biotech firm. The locals had found out the company had been testing its new and highly controversial vaccine illegally in the capital's slums, and they weren't pleased. Then again, maybe the attacks and the protests weren't really that different, since it was the vaccine that had caused the virus to mutate in the first place. Regardless of what was going on in Haiti, the virus didn't really take off until it reached Miami. I still wasn't quite clear about what had happened there, but then again, it seemed no one else was either. All I knew was that the infected and the infection had swept through the city within hours, forcing those who survived to flee. Some of them had been carrying the infection but were as yet unturned, which just spread the disease further and faster across the country.

Once I heard the rumours that the infected had reached Virginia I'd started preparing myself. At first, I stayed put. After all, it was what the Government was telling us to do, and I set to work collecting the recommended supplies: canned foods; bags of rice; water; medicines. I also joined the ill-tempered crowds that queued for fuel at the town's only gas station, and at the hardware store, for plywood to board up the windows. It was just like what happened whenever a hurricane threatened, only ten times worse. With hurricanes, people at least knew what they were dealing with. But with this disease, no one really knew what to expect.

As the virus, and the infected that carried it, grew ever closer, things started getting out of control. One evening as I was driving home, I saw the town's two deputies threatening a woman with their guns as her terrified kids huddled in the back of her car. It was clear they were after the food that filled every available space in her vehicle. By the time I'd passed, I could see her standing at the side of the road holding her kids and crying, as the police officers drove off: one in their patrol car, the other in hers. That was when I started thinking it might be an idea to get out before things got any worse, but I wanted to make sure this was the right thing to do. I figured I should sleep on it for the night before moving on. That turned out to be a big mistake, and I woke in the morning to find the first of the infected among us. I had been lucky: my apartment was on Main Street and I'd glanced through a crack between the boards I'd hastily nailed across the windows before going outside. What I saw shocked me. There were two people lying in the street, with others huddled round them. At first, I thought they were trying to help, then I realised they were clawing the people's torsos with their hands, and ripping off strips of flesh with their teeth. I watched, horror-struck, as the abdomen of first one person and then the other was torn open. Blood and guts spilled onto the dusty pavement, and I had to fight hard not to throw up.

Suddenly, a man appeared out of a side street, carrying a small child on his back. He had his head turned, talking to the toddler, so he didn't see the infected before they saw him. With a speed that was almost unbelievable, they leapt to their feet and raced towards them. They must have made a sound because his head suddenly snapped round. Seeing the infected descending on him, he froze for a moment before turning and running, but with the child on his back he barely moved faster than if he was walking. Glancing desperately over one shoulder then the other he saw the infected closing rapidly on him. Then he did the only thing that gave him a chance of escape: he dropped the child. Unencumbered, he finally started to draw away while two of the infected descended on the screaming child, biting and tearing at it until there was little left but scraps of blood-soaked clothing and scattered lumps of flesh. The only thing that was still recognisable was the head, and I could see the child's eyes frozen in terror as one of the infected gnawed on her left cheek.

At that moment, I knew if I didn't leave soon I'd never get out, but I needed a plan. I wracked my brains, trying to think of somewhere I could go where the infected wouldn't find me. Then, as if out of nowhere, the sign popped into my head. I knew these weren't really zombies, but surely if the virus had wiped out everything human within them, they mightn't remember how to swim. After all, swimming's not like walking or running, it didn't come naturally; it was something you had to specifically learn. With no other options coming to mind, I decided it was the best chance I had.

***

I slam on the brakes and the SUV skids to a halt at the end of the dirt track leading from the gates to the boat yard's single dock. I sit there with the engine idling, my eyes darting round nervously, trying to work out what to do next. There doesn't seem to be anyone around, so at least I shouldn't have to worry about infected. I don't really know anything about boats, so I don't know which one I should choose, or how I'm going to drive it, but I figure it can't be that much different from driving a car.

A movement in the rear-view mirror catches my eye; it's off in the distance and little more than dust being kicked up into the air, but it means something's coming this way. It might just be people trying to escape, but it could just as easily be infected, and I'm not going wait around to find out. Leaving the engine running and the door open, I leap from the car and run down to the wooden pontoon which stretches out into the water. Boats of all shapes and sizes are tied up there, and at first, I'm at a loss as to which one to take. Then I see it: a long, sleek speedboat with two huge engines on the back, and I know it's the one for me. I run to it and jump on board before racing over to the steering wheel. When I get there I'm surprised to find that you need a key and there's no obvious way to hot-wire it. I climb back onto the dock and scratch my head, wondering what I'm going to do now. As I do, I become aware of a noise that I can't quite place. It's; like the sound of water rushing over the edge of a massive waterfall and crashing into pool far below. Then I realise it's the sound of people, or more likely infected, pounding along the road towards me.

Growing ever more desperate, I try motorboat after motorboat, while all the time the noise grows louder and louder, but I can't get any of them started. Finally, right on the end of the dock, I see a sailboat, no more than twenty feet long, and I realise it's my salvation: I won't need any keys because I won't need to start the engine, all I'll need to do is raise the sails and I'll be away. I've never sailed before but I figure it can't be too difficult. I jump on board and just as I start untying the ropes I glance up to see the first of the infected entering the boatyard.

At first, they don't know where to go but they must have sensed my movements because before I know it, they're hurtling towards the dock. By the time I get the last rope free and have pushed the boat away from the shore, they're streaming along the pontoon, mouths open, roaring and snarling. I feel a gentle breeze on the back of my neck as I stare at them, both terrified and hypnotized by the sight of the infected sweeping towards me. The first of the infected reach the end of the pontoon and stop, while the ones behind them keep going, pushing those ahead of them into the water. I watch as they thrash around before sinking from sight. Just as the sign predicted: zombies can't swim.

Then I notice something. Little by little, I'm drifting back towards the dock. I'm not too sure what I should be doing but I figure I need to get the sails up. The mast seems a logical place to start since that's what the sails are attached to, so I run forward but find there's ropes everywhere and I can't work out which does what. I try pulling on them but nothing happens. I glance back desperately back to the pontoon. It's only ten feet away now and the closer I get, the more the infected are being whipped into a frenzy. I turn my attention back to the boat and I realise there are straps tied round the sail. I figure these are what's stopping me from pulling it up, so I frantically undo them one by one, stumble back to the mast and pull randomly on the ropes again. This time, I find one which raises the sail and I start pulling on it as hard as I can. The sail goes up and fills with wind but it pushes me towards the land I'm trying so hard to get away from. I let the rope go and with a crash the sail drops onto the deck. While the boat slows, it's still drifting inexorably towards the dock and the infected that wait for me there. That's when it finally dawns on me: while zombies can't swim, I can't sail, so it's not really going to help me survive after all.

***

Author's Note: This story was inspired by a photograph of a real sign I came across on the Web, which was genuinely used as advertising in a boatyard and proclaimed: '*Zombies can't swim. Get a Boat*'. Looking into this further, it seems such signs are not as uncommon as you might think. I don't know if several people have, independently, come up with the same slogan, or if there was one original sign which all the others copied, but either way, it struck me as a great title for a story, and it was one I couldn't resist writing.

Last Flight Out

I tapped the fuel gauge for the third time in five minutes. It made no difference: all it did was bounce on empty; I was running on fumes. One way or another I was going to end up back on the ground, and it would be soon. I circled round, looking desperately for somewhere I could set the plane down. At least it meant that if I crashed, or more likely when, I wouldn't have to worry about there being a fire. Then again, given how the world now was, fire was the least of my worries.

When I'd taken off a few hours before, I'd done it in a rush, and checking to see how much fuel was on board had hardly been my top priority, which was, instead, getting out alive. I'd watched the horde of infected sweep up the road from the town, drawn by the hum of the generators, and decided it was finally time to bug out. It wasn't like there was any one left to evacuate; well, not anyone who really mattered. The last of them had come through the day before and all the chatter over the radio suggested there'd be no more airlifts: not now; not ever. Both the refugees and the infected had been working their way northwards from Glasgow and the Central Belt for the last few days, ever since the outbreak had started, and now it seemed they were here.

I could hardly be accused of dereliction of duty for leaving when I did. I'd done my job; I'd kept the airport open, allowing as many of the soldiers and marines as possible to get out as they pulled back time and time again. The word on the ground was that Scotland was finished, and all efforts were being concentrated on defending the hastily-erected blockade at Hadrian's Wall. That was their grand plan for protecting the rest of the country. Despite the fact that there were still several million people there, all desperate for salvation, the north was being abandoned and the ancient Roman fortification revived, more than 1,500 years after it had last served any useful purpose. If the strategy was to have any chance of halting the advance of the infection, and the infected, they'd need every soldier they could get, and it had been my job to see that as many of those who'd been responsible for the failed containment in the north made it there in one piece. It had been Dunkirk in reverse, with everyone trying to get south rather than north. But this evacuation wasn't by boat, it was by air, and the enemy was so much worse.

When the last transporter had left the day before, I was promised they'd come back for me but when I'd put the call in, I was told was to hold my position ... just in case. Just in case of what, I didn't know, but that was when I realised I was being scarified for the greater good, along with everyone else north of the border. Right there and then, I started looking round for other options. It was only a small airport, so I had a choice of just three planes. The fact that I could only find the keys to one of them meant the decision had been made for me. It was a little four-seater Cessna; the kind where the wings were fixed above the windows.

I'd just starting to inspect the plane when I became aware of a noise in the distance. At first, it sounded like insects scurrying over fallen leaves, but as it grew louder it resolved itself into the sound of a multitude of feet pounding on tarmac. It took me a few minutes to get the plane going. By then, the infected were at the gates. There were thousands of them, all pushing and tearing at the chain-link fence surrounding the airport. It was the first time I'd seen them in person rather than on the news, but I'd heard the soldiers, the ones who had been on the front lines, talking about their wild eyes that seemed to burn with hatred and anger; about how they could be on you in seconds, tearing into you, ripping you apart, spilling your guts across the ground, while you screamed in agony. They wouldn't stop until you were dead.

This is what the virus did to you; the one which had started in Haiti and was now spreading around the world. It was worst when it was someone you knew, so the soldiers said. I'd heard them talk about it; about how they'd made pacts to finish each other off if they became infected, and couldn't do it for themselves. They'd rather die than become one of them. Yet, some of them had. I could see them in amongst those that were now surrounding me, easily visible in khaki uniforms stained with blood. The fence swayed and shuddered; it wouldn't hold, not for long at any rate. I revved the engine as the first section fell and they started to surge through. As I raced along the runway, the infected pursued me, the nearest almost reaching me as I lifted off. I was safe and now all I had to do was make it far enough south to cross the barricade. Then, and only then, would I be beyond their reach.

***

As I circled, I tried to work out exactly where I was. Off in the distance, I could just make out the newly resurrected fortifications of Hadrian's Wall. I wondered if I could make it, but it seemed too far. Instead, I turned my attention to the road directly below me, the one I'd been following for the last thirty minutes: the M74; the main artery that, until a day or so ago, had connected Scotland and England. One carriageway was jammed with the cars of people who'd tried to flee south to escape the outbreak, but the northbound one looked pretty clear. It was wide enough that I'd be able to set the plane down, but then what would I do? In amongst the cars I could see figures moving back and forth. From this height, they could have been mistaken for normal people, but while I couldn't quite work out what it was, there was something about the way they moved that told me they were infected. I'd just decided to try for the wall after all, when the engine spluttered for the first time. A minute later it spluttered again, and I was certain I wasn't going to make it. I was going down on the wrong side of the wall, whether I liked it or not.

With a final cough, the engine died and I was left gliding towards the ground. The silence was disconcerting as I looked around, trying to pick out a landing zone. I settled for a point on the road about a quarter of a mile ahead, and tried to prepare myself for the impact. That was when I noticed them: a group of about twenty, tracking my movements as my altitude dropped. I watched as more and more of them emerged from amongst the jammed cars on the other side of the road. I hoped I could outpace them and land with enough grace that I could make it out of the plane. If that happened, I was probably fit enough to make it to the wall before they got to me. I believed it. I had to. It was my only chance.

Sooner than expected, I felt the ground effect lift the plane ever so slightly. It told me I would be on the ground in seconds. I squirmed in my seat, trying to judge how far behind me the infected were. I figured about 300 yards. The wall was about a mile ahead; so close and yet so far away. I wondered how I was going to make it. I was fit, but I had little idea whether I really could outrun them over any sort of distance. Yet I had no choice. I pulled back on the stick and felt the rear wheels touch, followed by the front one. The plane bounced once and then again. As it settled down I saw a pothole ahead of me. I twisted the stick to the left, but with no power I had little hope of avoiding it. I missed the hole with the front wheel but the one on the left-hand side at the back struck it, sending the plane spinning towards the central reservation, and the steel barriers which lined it. I slammed on the brakes, but it was too little too late. There was a sickening crunch as the front wheel buckled, sending the nose crashing into the ground. My head smashed into the dashboard and I blacked out for a second. When I came to, I could feel blood dripping down the side of my face. It took me a moment to work out where I was. Then I remembered the infected. I glanced out of the left-hand window and saw them appearing over the brow of a small hill to my north. I tried to open the right-hand door, but it was jammed. I put my shoulder to it and found it wouldn't budge. I tried the other one. It swung open easily, but that was when I realised I couldn't move: my legs were trapped.

I turned back to the infected. They were closer now, and I could hear them: the noise something between a roar and a growl that sank deep into my soul. I looked at my legs. The right one wasn't badly trapped, but there was no way I was getting the left one free; a large piece of metal had pierced my thigh and blood poured from the wound. Even if I could pull it out, I'd bleed to death before I got anywhere near the wall, and I'd never be able to move faster than the infected.

I pulled the door shut again and flipped the latch. I closed my eyes and listened. Over the sound of my heart pounding in my ears I could hear the infected as they raced towards me. With panic bubbling up in my stomach, I tried to work out how many there were. I couldn't get an exact number, just the impression that there were a lot. I opened my eyes and stared down at my legs again. Then an idea came to me: a trick an old medic had once told me about. I looked around for something I could use. The only suitable thing was the seatbelt. I felt around for my penknife and then used it to cut the seatbelt into a long, thick strap. I wrapped it round my leg, higher up than the metal and tied it as tight as I could get it. Next, I took a screwdriver from amongst the tools which had spilled onto the floor of the plane in the crash and pushed it between the strap and my leg before twisting it to tighten the makeshift tourniquet as far as it would go. I gripped the metal and took a deep breath. The pain as I pulled it free was so blinding I almost passed out again, but somehow I kept it together. I looked at the gaping hole it had left behind as it slowly filled with blood. No gushing. No spurting. Just seeping. That was about as good as I could hope for. It looked like the tourniquet was doing its job, at least for the moment.

There was a sudden bang on the side of the Cessna, somewhere back near the tail. I glanced up. The first of the infected had reached me, and there was no longer any chance of escape. I felt the plane start to rock as others arrived. Then the first one drew level with the window. He stared at me for a moment. He was tall and thin, and dressed in a light grey suit that was now little more than rags. He'd lost a shoe somewhere and his face and hair were caked with dirt. He looked human, but there was no hint of humanity behind his eyes. Instead, they burned with rage. He screamed and threw himself at the glass, pummelling it until his knuckles were bleeding. More and more appeared with every passing second until I was surrounded. Some climbed onto the nose and started banging on the windscreen. It had already cracked in the crash and they would be through it in no time.

I felt for the holster which was strapped to my side. Finding it, I pulled out the pistol a departing soldier had given me, as a thank you for my help. It felt heavy in my hand. I lined it up with the first of them; a young woman, maybe in her early twenties. She showed no fear, or hint of recognition that a gun was pointed at her head. She just kept pounding on the windscreen. I'd never fired a gun before but at this range I could barely miss. I paused for a moment, trying not to think about what I was about to do, and then slowly tightened my finger on the trigger. The noise inside the confines of the cockpit was deafening and the gun almost jerked from my hand. As if in slow motion, the girl's head exploded as she fell backwards off the plane and crumpled to the ground. I felt sickened by what I'd done, but knew I'd had no choice. None of the others seemed to care or even notice. Gripping the gun more firmly, I lined up the next shot and fired again, and then again. For a moment, the windscreen was clear, and it crossed my mind to try to scramble out, but before I could move another clambered up ... followed by a second ... and a third. My ears were still ringing from the shots, but I could still hear the infected as they hammered on the fuselage all around me, making it jump and shudder.

I heard glass breaking and turned to see the window on the left had given out. The man in the tattered suit was trying to clamber in, his grasping arms reaching towards me. I fired twice, missing him both times. The third time I finally hit him and he slumped where he lay, half in and half out of the window. I left his body hanging there in the hope it might stop others following him in. The windscreen shattered, sending two infected tumbling into the cockpit. I stared at them, frozen with fear as they scrambled to get to me. Then a realisation washed over me: there was only one option left. As I pressed the barrel against my head, I felt their hands tearing at my torso and their teeth biting into my flesh. I was surprised by how little it hurt. My hand shook and I hesitated, but I knew it was the only way out. I took deep breath, knowing it would be over the instant I did it ... and pulled the trigger.

***

Author's Note: The idea behind this story popped into my head when I was watching a small plane fly over my house while I sat in the back garden. What, I wondered, would it be like to be up there in the sky, looking down at a zombie apocalypse? You would have a completely different perspective of it than those stuck on the ground, because you'd be able to see so much. You would also feel somewhat divorced from it all, with the hordes of zombies looking more like ants than people.

I then started wondering about what would happen once the plane started running low on fuel. Where would the pilot land? What would happen to them? How would they feel as they descended towards the zombie hordes waiting for them far below. It was from these thoughts that this story was born.

This story also introduces the idea of building military walls to keep zombies back. Walls, even to this day, have always served important military purposes, and in this case, I liked the idea of resurrecting one of the two ancient Roman walls which once cut the island of Great Britain in two. This issue is explored in more detail in another story in this book, called *The Wall*. It also forms, in passing, part of one of the themes within the sequel to *For those in Peril on the Sea*, on which I'm currently working: namely, how the military would respond to a zombie apocalypse, and whether they would do what had to be done, regardless of the cost to civilians and even their own soldiers.

Waiting Up For Santa Claus:
A Cautionary Tale

'Look!' the girl pointed excitedly. 'It's him. It has to be.'

The boy glanced at the clock on the wall, slightly confused, 'But it's not midnight yet.'

'So?'

'So, it's not Christmas Day, is it?'

'But it looks just like him. And besides,' the girl said knowingly, 'it's already Christmas somewhere. Maybe he's just early.'

The two children were peeking through their curtains, trying not to be seen. Despite their mother's frequent warnings that he wouldn't come unless they were asleep, they were determined to catch a glimpse of Santa Claus. They tried every year but had never quite managed it. This year, it seemed, they might have finally succeeded. At five minutes to twelve, they'd heard a noise and had scampered from their beds to investigate.

Outside, their front yard was covered with snow; the snowman they'd built earlier in the day still staring off into the distance. Beside him was a new figure, his red coat stretched across his portly belly. They couldn't see his face, but curly white hair hung down below a hat edged with fur. Beside the man lay a large sack from which spilled brightly wrapped packages. He stood slouching, one arm around the neck of the snowman. The man wasn't really moving, just swaying slightly from side to side.

The boy glanced up at his sister. 'What should we do?'

The older child scratched her head as she surveyed the room they'd shared for as long as either of them could remember. A Christmas tree stood decorated in one corner, while home-made streamers were strung across the ceiling. Finally, her eyes landed on the stockings that hung expectantly from the ends of their beds, and an idea popped into her head. She grinned at her brother, 'Let's go out and see if he'll give us our presents now, before we go to sleep.'

'Yeah, that would be really cool.'

'We'll need to be quiet though. We don't want Mom waking up.'

The younger kid rubbed his backside, remembering how it had felt when he'd been spanked for getting into a fight at school. If she'd been mad because of that, she'd be madder if she caught them out of bed on Christmas Eve. She'd already shouted at them earlier in the evening, when they were still bouncing round their room long after they should have been tucked up in bed ... twice. But this was an opportunity not to be missed. After all, how many other kids would be able to say they'd got their presents from Santa Claus himself, rather than just waking up on Christmas morning and finding he'd visited them in the night?

They grabbed their stockings and crept to the door. The elder child inched it open, making sure it didn't squeak. Once there was enough room, they slipped through and snuck down the stairs, remembering to jump over the loose one at the bottom; the one that always creaked loudly when anyone stood on it. At the front door, the girl turned to her younger brother. 'You sure about this?'

He nodded enthusiastically.

She reached up and took the key from its hook before sliding it into the keyhole. It first turned smoothly and silently, then there was resistance, followed by a quiet click, which told her the door was now unlocked. The girl pressed down the handle and pulled it open, letting in a blast of frigid air. The two children shivered in their thin night-clothes. Outside, the street was silent, the snow muffling the usual noises of the night. The man had moved away from the snowman and now stood on the far side of their front yard with his back to them. The snow round his feet was messed up, as if he'd been shuffling through it rather than walking across it. His sack still lay on the ground by the snowman, seemingly forgotten.

Leaving the door open, the girl stepped forward, feeling the snow crunch under her weight, the cold shooting up through the soles of her feet. For a moment, she thought about going back for her shoes, but that would take time and he might be gone before she got back. She'd just need to be quick. Running forward, she called out quietly, 'Santa, don't go. We're here. Can we have our presents now?'

Just as the girl reached the snowman, the figure in the red suit turned and she saw his face for the first time. She skidded to a halt, causing her brother to crash into her from behind, and stared at the face beneath the fur-trimmed hat. The man's pale, sallow skin was splattered with red and his white beard was stained by a thick dark fluid that dripped slowly onto the snow. His deeply sunken eyes were a dull black with no spark of life in them.

'That's not Santa Claus, is it?' There was a frightened tone in the young boy's voice. He clung to his sister's arm. He didn't know why but the man scared him. Maybe it was something to do with the eyes and the way they seemed to stare right through him.

'No.' The girl was frightened too. She tried to think of what to do next, but it seemed her brain had stopped working. She wanted to run, but couldn't; she was rooted to the spot.

Then the man started towards them, slowly at first, but becoming faster with each faltering step. Suddenly, the girl was no longer frozen with fear. She turned and fled, pulling her younger brother with her, but it was difficult to run across the snow in bare feet. She glanced over her shoulder and saw that the man in the Santa outfit was gaining on them. As he moved, he let out a moan which sank deep into her soul.

The kids were almost back at the house when the girl's foot slipped on a patch of ice. She tumbled to the ground, pulling her little brother with her and landing heavily on her back. She pushed the boy onwards, towards the safety of the front door. As he disappeared inside, the girl rolled onto her front. The snow crumbled beneath her as she struggled to get back onto her feet.

The girl yelled when she felt the man's hand close around her leg and start dragging her backwards through the snow. But it didn't feel like a real hand. While it gripped her so tightly it hurt, there was no warmth in it. Instead, it felt as cold as ice. She turned and saw the man's face again, this time much closer. His red hat had fallen from his head, but he didn't seem to have noticed or even to care. While his eyes looked lifeless, maybe even soulless, his jaw moved back and forth, causing his teeth to gnash against each other.

The girl kicked out, trying to break his grip, but even though she hit him as hard as she could, he didn't seem to notice. She heard someone screaming. It seemed distant at first, but quickly grew closer and closer. For a moment, the girl wondered who it was. Then it dawned on her that the sound was coming from her own mouth. She struggled frantically, but it was no use. She couldn't get away. As the figure in the red suit loomed over her, blocking out the stars, the girl felt his fetid breath on the side of her face and realised she was going to die.

The man sank his teeth deep into her neck, ripping at her flesh. Although the girl could see her own blood spraying across the snow-covered yard, turning it a deep crimson red, she felt no pain. As the life drained from her body, the girl wished she'd listened to her mother. She wished she'd gone to sleep instead of trying to stay awake until Santa Claus arrived.

***

Author's Note: This story was written as a Christmas 'thanks' to the readers of my blog (*cmdrysdale. wordpress.com*). It builds on the tradition of Christmas horror stories, and also on the fact that, at one time or another, every child has tried to stay up long enough to catch a glimpse of Santa Claus, despite the dire warnings from their parents that he wouldn't come while they were still awake. This story provides yet another reason why it's unwise to try this.

Nightwatch

There's the smell of decomposing flesh in the still night air, but I've got no sense of how long it has been there. I adjust my grip on the spade I'm holding. I sniff again. Is it my imagination or is it getting stronger? A twig cracks behind me. I turn and swing. I catch a glimpse of a face, cheeks rotting and teeth bared, just before the spade obliterates it. I stare at the fetid corpse, shocked at how close the zombie had got undetected. My lesson learned, I swear to myself I'll never fall asleep on watch again.

The Watcher[2]

Through a gap between the shutters I watch the zombies stagger ever closer and wonder if our defences can withstand yet another attack.

Leaving

I move from the barricaded windows, back towards our bed, and kiss her as she sleeps. I've loved her for as long as I can remember, but now I'm abandoning her when she needs me most. I look down again at the now-festering bite mark on my arm. How could I have been so careless?

---

[2] This is a piece of Twitter fiction, which aims to tell a whole story within the 140 characters allowed in a single 'Tweet'.

The Lighthouse At The End Of The Road

The dog's ears prick up and he growls quietly, but whatever it is that's caught his attention it's not enough to make him sit up. Instead, he remains lying on his side in front of the glowing embers in the fireplace. I reach over and scratch him behind his left ear as he falls silent again. A second later, he's on his feet, facing the door, hackles raised, a deep rumble coming from his throat. Now I know he's sensed something out there in the darkness, I hope it's only a fox and not one of *them*. This is my third hideout in four weeks, each more remote than the last. If we have to leave, I don't know where we'd go from here. Surrounded by sea on three sides, the lighthouse is about as far from civilisation as I can get. Right up on the north-west tip of Scotland, it's miles from anywhere and any human habitation. There isn't even a road here, just a track which starts at a small pier on a narrow inlet and ends at the lighthouse itself. We'd had to leave the car on the other side of the water, walk round the end and then onwards up the last ten miles. I can't see how any of *them* could have made it here, not yet anyway. The dog steps backwards, one leg at a time and growls again, ears up, lips curled back, head down, sniffing at the wind whistling under the door, trying to get a scent of whatever it is he hears out there. This is what he was like just before the last place was overrun.

There'd been five of us there, but only me and the dog had made it out alive, and that was only because his superior senses gave me just enough advance warning before they'd attacked. I'd learned from the first safe house that to stay and fight was a sure way to end up dead, so I'd started scrambling for the back door the moment I realised why he was acting strangely. Before I could warn the others the first of *them* came crashing through the door. Jen and Mike had been killed before they made it out of their sleeping bags. Jack got as far as the kitchen, and Sam was just behind me when they grabbed him. That extra second, that extra foot the dog's warning had given me, was what had made the difference between escape and death. Even though I'd only known them for a week, I'd liked those guys, and it was devastating to know they were now gone. As I'd driven away, I'd sworn to myself I wasn't going to get attached to anyone else again. From then on, it was always going to be just me and the dog.

The dog barked. I'd tried to get him to stop doing that ever since I'd found him wandering along an otherwise empty road, but it seemed it's just part of his nature. This was before I met up with Mike and his friends. I'd been on my own for three days by that point, and I'd been glad of the company. The dog felt the same way, and once he'd sniffed me enough to be certain I wasn't one of *them,* he was all over me. Since then, regardless of whether we were somewhere nice and warm or out in the open, we'd barely left each other's side. I'd only been on that road because of what had happened at the first place I'd found myself in.

When the dead started to rise and attack the living, those of us who were prepared, grabbed our gear and ran. I chose to head north to where there were fewer people, and so fewer bodies to crawl from what were meant to be their final resting places. After a couple of days, I'd found myself at a farmhouse set into the hills above Loch Ness, along with nineteen or twenty others, all refugees from places further south: Fort William, Perth, Dundee, Glasgow, Edinburgh. There'd even been a couple who'd managed to make it all the way up from Newcastle without getting killed which, given the circumstances, was pretty impressive.

The farmhouse lasted two weeks before the dead started turning up, shambling along the track leading to the front door, or over the grass-covered hill behind it. I don't know where they came from, or what attracted them to us, but they came nonetheless. At first, they only came in ones and twos, and we could keep them under control, but gradually, the numbers built and we found it more and more difficult to stay on top of the situation. Then came the night they breached our defences. We started to fight back, but very quickly it became clear this was a losing strategy, and it wasn't long before the few of us who survived more than a couple of minutes turned and fled. This was no organised retreat. It was pure panic; each of us simply picked a direction and ran, hoping we wouldn't crash headlong into any of *them* in the darkness. Some probably died, but others, like me, must have got lucky and made it out. If they did, I'd never find out, because I knew I'd never see any of them again.

After that, I always made sure I had an exit strategy, no matter where I found myself. At least, I had until I'd reached the lighthouse at the end of the road. It was so remote and I was so tired that when I'd arrived, just as the sun was going down, I figured I could wait until the morning to scope out the place in full. Now, with the dog growling beside me, I quickly scanned the room. There were three windows in the circular room which formed the base of the lighthouse, but none of them were big enough for me to crawl through. I cursed myself for mistakenly thinking I'd be safe here, but I still couldn't work out where any dead could have come from. As far as I knew, no one had lived this far out since the lighthouse had been automated, nearly thirty years ago, but then again, maybe I hadn't been the only one to think it might be the ultimate safe house. Someone could have been injured by one of the risen dead and made it here, or close to it, before finally succumbing to whatever it was that was passed on when one of them bit you.

There was another snarl followed by a short, sharp bark. I tried to keep him quiet by holding his muzzle but he struggled free and barked again. There was definitely something out there, but I didn't know what, and there was no way I was opening the door to find out. All I could do was crouch beside my faithful companion and hope it was not one of *them*.

***

Author's Note: The Cape Wrath Lighthouse, where this story is set, marks the north-western tip of the Scottish mainland, and while this part of the country was more heavily inhabited before the Clearances, it's now one of the most sparsely populated regions of Western Europe. This would make it an appealing location to anyone trying to survive in a zombie apocalypse. If you want to find out more about where it is you can follow this link to see its location on Google Earth: http://www.forthoseinperil.net/_files/The_Lighthouse_At_ The_End_Of_The_Road.kmz (this requires that you have either Google Earth or the Google Earth Mobile app installed on your e-book device). Since 2009, there's been a café there, called the *Ozone Café*, so it's no longer completely uninhabited (as it was when I was growing up). On the cafe's website, there's a statement that's so at odds with the modern world, it only serves to emphasize its isolation: 'Unfortunately, due to the remoteness of The Ozone Café, an e-mail address is unavailable.' (quoted from http://www.capewrath.org.uk/ 10_Ozone_Cafe.htm).

A theme within this story is the benefit of having a dog as a companion in a zombie apocalypse. A dog would almost certainly give you advance warning of any approaching undead, but you may find their tendency to bark at inappropriate moments only serves to draw the walking dead to you. Personally, I think the benefits would outweigh the risks, but it would very much depend on the individual dog you had with you.

Oddly, this story was inspired directly by real events; not the zombie bits, but the actions of the dog. At one point in my life, I stayed in a remote lighthouse on an island in the Bahamas (the one at Hole-in-the-Wall on Abaco), and for a while, I was there alone, with the exception of a pair of dogs (or 'potcakes' as the local strays are called, which are a mix of every breed that's ever visited the islands). One of them had the unnerving habit of suddenly scrambling to her feet in the middle of the night before standing stock-still, staring towards the door, growling menacingly. After a minute or so, she'd lie down again as if nothing had happened, but it always made me wonder what she was sensing out there, in the darkness, that I couldn't detect.

The Wall

I stand, staring north along the broad road, as it disappears off into the distance. I'd always wanted to visit Scotland, but now this is as close as I'll ever get; it's as close as I'd ever want to get. Infected swarm around the base of the wall which has become our latest line of defence against them. I hope it will hold; we all do. It's our last chance of keeping the disease contained.

I hear the sound of an engine racing even above the groaning and shuffling of the infected that push against the wall in their hundreds, possibly even thousands. Those are just the ones I can see, and I've no idea how many others there might be out there, attacking the wall along its seventy-three-mile length.

I search for the vehicle, but it takes me a while to find it; an RV, off in the distance, hurtling down the deserted northbound carriageway of the M74; the road which once connected Scotland and England, and that the wall now cuts in two. I wonder how they've survived so long out there in what has become the 'Badlands', or where they think they're going. Surely they must know that even if they make it past all the infected, we can't let them through?

Not wanting to watch what will happen to those inside, I turn away and light a cigarette. The smoking's new. Before, I'd always been scared of getting cancer, but now there are worse things to worry about — much worse — and anyway, it gives me something to do with my hands while I'm on guard duty; just like drinking does when I'm off. I watch the end of the cigarette glow as smoke spirals up into the sky, and I wonder at how much the world has changed in such a short space of time.

***

There'd been outbreaks all over the world, but ours had started in Glasgow the week before. At first, they'd tried to contain it there, but the soldiers on the barricades couldn't easily distinguish the infected from those who were just trying to flee and, anyway, there weren't enough of them to stop the mass of people that wanted to get out. They'd seen on the news the day before what'd happened in Miami when the infection, and the infected, overran the city, and they weren't about to wait round for the same thing to happen to Glasgow. That just made the job of containment all the more difficult for those on the front lines. In fact, it was impossible.

I think the generals must have known this from the start, because even before they'd ordered the first pullback, they'd set us to work resurrecting the ancient wall. Originally, it had been built to guard the northern frontier of the mighty Roman Empire against wild Pictish warriors, who tried again and again to expel it from their homeland. Now, we'd rebuilt it to keep at bay a much more frightening enemy: a virus. It didn't sound scary until you saw what it made people do to each other: it took over their brains and their bodies; extinguishing all traces of who they'd once been; turning them into something altogether different. Driven to pass it on, the infected would attack anyone without the virus, but often they'd go too far: killing them, tearing them apart, even eating them.

That was what happened if the infected found you one-on-one, but if they got into a crowd it was different. All those people running around, panicking, screaming and shouting, it seemed to confuse them. They'd attack one person, but only long enough to bring them down before running after another, then another. In crowds, they wouldn't kill. Instead, they'd just infect. This allowed the virus to spread, and spread rapidly. That's what had happened in Glasgow, and what was now happening everywhere north of the wall.

When we were rebuilding the wall, it seemed like almost every soldier and reservist in the country was there. Well, all those not fighting the infected directly on the front line. Whether they knew it or not, their job wasn't really containment, as was reported on the news, but rather to slow the spread of the virus and buy us enough time to get what we hoped would be our new frontier finished. Yes, the generals were condemning anyone north of the wall to death, or worse, but what choice did they have? They were sacrificing five million but they were doing it to save sixty. It was a tough decision, but it was the right one; the only logical one.

It was amazing to watch the wall go up. Twenty-five feet high and ten feet wide, it had a scaffolding skeleton lined with almost anything we could get our hands on: plywood, tarpaulins, sand bags, bales of hay, anything that would hold back the rocks, the rubble, the earth and the sand we filled it with. Like the Romans before us, we used the natural features of the land to help make the defences as impregnable as possible. In some cases, we even used the remains of the Roman wall itself to help speed up the construction, but unlike the Romans, we didn't need to worry about gateways or forts. Once it was completed, no one was going to be allowed through from the north, no matter what.

We completed it in two days, but with nearly 30,000 of us working on it, it wasn't nearly as impressive as it sounds. That was when they started what they called a 'phased withdrawal'. Well, that's what they were calling it for us. To the media and the public they were still talking about 'containment'. They airlifted the troops out, starting with the ones closest to the action, but left the civilians behind. Three days later, even that stopped: it was getting too risky. By then, the gradual trickle of people fleeing southwards from the infected had grown into a raging torrent, but we had to hold firm. We couldn't tell who might be infected, but as yet unturned, and who was infection-free. And there was no way we could risk the virus getting through the wall. As far as I knew, there was no Plan B, so if that happened, the whole country was finished … that was how important the wall was.

If the ever-building crowds came too close to the wall, we'd fire warning shots to keep them away. It was heartbreaking to see them: men, women, whole families all trying to get away from the infection, but there was nothing any of us could do. As we watched helplessly, they set up makeshift camps all along the northern edge of the wall; some with tents, others making use of cars, caravans and whatever else they could find. At night, I could see thousands upon thousands of fires, burning in the darkness, stretching as far as the eye could see, both along the wall and off into the north.

Then the infected started to appear. I don't know where they came from. Maybe they'd followed those trying to flee south, or maybe it was people who'd been bitten and had got this far, before finally losing their battle against the virus. At first, we tried to take them out, shooting at anyone who had clearly turned before they could attack too many others. When it was an adult it wasn't too hard, but when it was a teenager or, even worse, a child, it was gut-wrenchingly difficult. Yet it had to be done. Even then it didn't really make a difference, because soon there were just too many of them. Pandemonium broke out amongst the refugees. It was horrific watching all those people as the infection and the infected surged through the crowds below the wall, but I couldn't take my eyes off them. No one knew what to do; where to go. Some tried to climb the wall or tear it down, and we were ordered to shoot them. Others called up to where we stood, asking for our help, or holding up their children, pleading for us to save them. Even if we'd been allowed, they were too far below to reach without risking our own lives, and none of us were willing to do that. Then, there were the ones that ran. They didn't know where they were heading, they just took off and when one person started, others around them would follow, turning a frightened mob into a stampede that swept across all in its path. Anyone who fell or got in its way was trampled underfoot.

That night almost no fires burned in the darkness, and by dawn there were none. As the sun rose it revealed what was left of the refugee camps. Gone were the clusters of tents and people. In the night they'd been replaced by a roaring, swirling sea of infected. They lined the wall, forty or fifty deep, all trying to get to the uninfected they could sense on the other side. They attacked the makeshift structure, beating and tearing at it until their hands bled.

***

As I finish my cigarette, I hear the RV screech to a halt. I turn to find it's now close enough to the wall that the occupants must be able to make out the swarm of infected which line it as far as the eye can see. I watch as it sits there, its engine idling, and I wonder what the driver's thinking. The engine roars again and the RV leaps forward. When it reaches the first of the infected it doesn't slow; it just ploughs through them. It doesn't even slow as it approaches the wall itself. Instead, it slams into it. I feel a tremor pass under my feet. For a moment, I wonder if the wall will hold, but then I realise that one RV would have little impact on the tons of earth and rock on which I stand. I peer over the edge and see the infected crowding around the vehicle, trying their best to get in. Then the skylight on its roof opens and a pair of hands appear. A moment later, they're followed by a head and then the rest of a young boy. Soon another person appears, then another and another. The last must have been the driver because he's bleeding from a gash across his face, which looks like it's been caused by his head hitting the steering wheel. They glance around frantically, seeing that the RV is surrounded by infected on three sides whilst the front end is crumpled against the wall. They're only a few feet below me, but before they can do anything the RV shudders, causing one of the kids to lose his footing. As he scrambles back to his feet, the vehicle starts to sway violently as the infected attack it, trying to get to the people huddled on its roof.

Shielding his eyes with his hand, the man looks up and sees me watching from the top of the wall. He's got a scrawny beard and lank, unwashed hair. There's dirt ingrained into the lines on his face and his clothes are stained and grubby. At first, I'm disgusted. Then it occurs to me that I probably look pretty much the same to him. He calls out.

'Hey, can you help us up?' His accent's Scottish, but I can't narrow it down any further than that.

'No.' It sounds harsh, but we have our orders.

'But you've got to,' the man urges me.

'The sergeant made it very clear. We can't help anyone from north of the wall.'

'Are you just going to stand there and watch them kill us?' the woman shouts incredulously. Her dark hair's tied back in a ponytail, revealing a pale, pinched face and sunken brown eyes. The two boys hiding between the adults are caked in dirt, and are so skinny it looks like a light breeze would blow them away. I'm guessing survival rather than food has been the number one priority for this family since the outbreak started.

I turn and walk a few feet away from the edge of the wall to give me time to think.

'Hey, come back! You can't just leave us here. Come back!' There's fear in the woman's voice and the kids start crying.

I blot this out as I try to work out what to do. It would be directly disobeying orders if I helped them, but unlike all the others I could reach these survivors without risking my own neck. Surely I couldn't let them get torn apart right there in front of me?

Suddenly there's a scream. I run forward and look down. The weight of the infected pushing on the RV is now so great that it's rocking wildly from side to side. In the commotion, the smaller of the two boys has been thrown from his feet and is now dangling over the edge of the roof. One of the taller infected has hold of his legs and is pulling the boy towards his gaping mouth. The only thing stopping the boy being dragged into the horde is the fact his mother and father have a hold of his arms and are pulling him upwards. The boy's screaming, both in pain and in fear. Without thinking I shoulder my rifle and shoot the infected through the head. Instantly, the boy is released, sending his parents tumbling on to the RV's roof as they finally get him clear.

Lying on his back, the man looks up at me hopefully. 'Does that mean you're going to help us?'

'I haven't decided yet.' I pause for a moment so I can think. 'How do I know you're not infected?'

'We're not. We're all okay.'

'That's what everyone says; even those who've been bitten.'

'But we are. How can we prove it to you?

'You can't.'

'So you're just going to leave us here?'

'There's nothing else I can do.'

'There must be something you can do!' The woman sounds desperate.

The RV tips sharply to its left, sending them all sprawling across its roof. This time, only the man and the younger of the two children manage to hold on. First, the older boy and then the woman slip over the edge and disappear into the arms of the infected waiting below. Blood and guts fly in all directions as the infected tear the screaming mother and child to pieces. The man gets up, but the RV is shuddering so wildly he's having trouble staying on his feet. There're tears streaming down his face.

'Please. You've got to help us. Or if not me, at least help him.' He points to where the boy's clinging to the roof. 'He's not injured, I promise you. He's clean. You can check for yourself once you get him up there. Look.' He pulls the boy to his feet and jerks up his jacket and shirt before spinning him round and round. I can see there are no bites on his slight torso.

I avoid the man's eyes, 'I can't. How would I explain where he came from?'

'I don't know, but surely you must be able to think of something?' he shouts desperately.

The RV tips again and I can see from his face that the man knows it's only a matter of time. He grabs the boy and holds him up. His eyes meet mine, 'Please. Save him.'

Against my better judgement, I sling my rifle across my back as I throw myself down and lean over the edge of the wall. I stretch my hands down towards the boy, but he's too frightened to reach up and grab them. The RV lurches and the man only just manages to stay upright.

'Come on, boy, take my hands,' I shout as I slide as far forward as I dare. 'Please,' I say more softly and then smile.

This seems to do the trick and he unfolds his arms. I feel his tiny hands close on mine just as the man finally loses his footing and falls, yelling, from the RV. The boy squirms, trying to see what's happened to his father.

Below him, I can see the man being ripped apart by the infected. 'Don't look down, boy, just look at me. You're almost safe. I'll have you up here in a jiffy, and then you'll be safe.'

Behind me, I hear the distinctive click of a bullet being chambered in an assault rifle. 'You'll do no such thing, soldier!'

I know the voice and I know I'm screwed. 'But, Sergeant, I can't just let him go.'

'Well, you can't bring him up here either. It's too risky. What if he's infected?'

I glance down at the boy. The left sleeve of his jacket has slipped and I can see blood on his forearm. I can't tell if it's from a bite, but it's definitely blood. Yet this is a living, breathing little boy. I can't just drop him into the mass of infected that are seething around the base of the wall, the nearest reaching their arms up towards him. I can see tears welling up in his frightened eyes as they silently plead with me to pull him to safety. I don't know what to do next: no matter what, I know it'll be the wrong decision for someone. All I can do is lie there, unable to decide one way or the other, the terrified boy dangling from my arms, the Sergeant standing behind me, his gun pointed at the back of my head and the infected swarming below.

***

Author's Note: This story is connected to an earlier one in this volume called *Last Flight Out*. In that story, the concept of rebuilding Hadrian's Wall (which is the name of the Roman wall that used to separate modern day Scotland and England more than 1,700 years ago) is introduced for the first time. Both of these stories are based on extra ideas I had while working on the first draft of the sequel to *For those in Peril on the Sea*. They didn't really fit into the main story, which is about a group of people escaping from the city of Glasgow during the very early stages of an outbreak of this virus, but I found them intriguing enough that I wanted to do something with them, rather than just abandoning them altogether.

If you want to see where Hadrian's Wall is and also see the exact location where this story is set, you can download a map overlay that will allow you to plot these on Google Earth from http://www.forthoseinperil.net/_files/The_Wall.kmz. In order to view this overlay, you have to have either Google Earth or the Google Earth Mobile app installed on your computer or e-book device. These are free and you can find the one that's best for you by entering the phrase 'Google Earth' into an Internet search engine.

The Girl At Little Harbour

Will's dead. I know he is. Although I'm doing my best not to look, I know if turn my head I'll be able to see his body lying where it fell after I'd finished smashing the oar against his skull. I killed him, but he killed me too; or at least as good as ... maybe even worse. Of all of them that had to be out there, why did it have to be him? I know it wasn't his fault, that it wasn't really him, just his body, driven by the virus that's changed the world so dramatically in the last few months. I don't know how many months exactly. It seems like forever, yet the summer's still not over, so it can't be more than four or five. I can't clearly remember the world as it was before. The memories are still there, but it's as if I see them through a haze or smoke or something. It's only the ones from after *it* happened that are clear now. At first, we called it *the disease*; *the outbreak*; *the end of the world*; and many other things. But at some point, we started calling it *it*, and that's the name which stuck.

I think of Carol-Lynn, my little girl, my beautiful baby. We called her Carol after Will's mother and Lynn after mine. It seemed logical at the time, but we might have come up with something different if we'd realised how much confusion it would cause. No one ever seemed to get it right, not at first anyway, and Carol-Lynn was very sensitive to the many mistakes. Every time someone got it wrong, she'd pout and give them a look that could curdle milk. Staring straight at them she'd say in a stern voice, 'My name's Carol-Lynn, not Carolyn or Carol-Anne, or Caroline, but Carol ...' she'd leave the slightest pause for emphasis, 'Lynn!' She'd been doing it pretty much since her first day at elementary school. I don't know where she got that look from, but Will always said it was the same look I gave him when he did something stupid. I smile when I remember this, and then cry again. How could it all end this way? Our perfect little family ripped apart, destroyed: Will dead, because I'd had to kill him; me infected; and Carol-Lynn ... What would happen to her?

There are other survivors around here. I know there are. That's why we'd come this far north, trying desperately to find others like ourselves, but will they find her before it's too late? How can they? They're not looking for her, why would they? They don't even know she exists. As long as she does as I've told her, she'll be safe and she has plenty of food, so maybe there's a chance. The other survivors aren't that far away, just a few more miles, and maybe one day soon, they'll come this way and find her.

I'll be long gone by then. Not dead, but turned into one of them; an infected, just like Will had been, but I have no one to put me out of my misery. I'm destined to roam, no longer really human, for god knows how long, attacking any survivors who come near. I don't know when, but sooner or later I'll turn and I can't be anywhere near Carol-Lynn, safely tucked away as she is, when that happens. I can't go to her and hug her one last time. I can't tell her I love her; that I'm sorry to be leaving her like this. I can't even say goodbye. When I don't come back as promised, she'll know something has happened to me. She won't know what, but she'll know that I've left her all alone in this terrifying and dangerous world, which none of us could have ever have foreseen.

***

We were in Trinidad when *it* happened. It started slowly, with rumours of strange things happening in Haiti, then in some of the other islands to the north. A while after that, someone with the infection turned up in Miami. That was when I started taking it seriously, but I figured the Government, the Center for Disease Control or someone, would work out a way to deal with it. I still didn't realise how bad it was; what this new virus did to people; and what it made them do to others. Then, out of nowhere, Miami was overrun. All I could do was stare at the television in the marina office along with everyone else, as we watched it happen. We had family and friends there and I tried calling, but the phone lines were jammed. All I could do was hope they'd made it out.

At first, the authorities spoke with confidence about dealing with it, but by the next day, the confidence had started to disappeared, replaced by confusion and fear. They didn't say it, but it was written across their faces. Then the virus jumped: to Britain; to Canada; to Rio. Within a few days, it seemed like it was everywhere.

The moment we heard the rumours of an outbreak on the island, we left. Along with five other yachts, all with families like ours on them, we set out, not really knowing where we were going, just that we needed to get away. Gradually, we meandered north, moving from island to island, looking for somewhere that was still safe. As we did, we watched the news reports with disbelief as the world fell apart. Then, right in the middle of a broadcast, the news channel stopped. We tried to find another one, but all we got was automated messages telling of technical problems, and falsely promising the shows would be right back. We tried the FM radio, but there was nothing on that either. Suddenly, it seemed like we were all alone in the world. Our little flotilla had reached the Turks and Caicos Islands by then, and there seemed little point in carrying on. Instead, we found an uninhabited island and set ourselves up there. To call it an island was perhaps a bit of wishful thinking as it was really just a very large sandbank that rose about ten feet above the water, covered with scrubby bushes, but there was no risk of running into anyone with the infection so we were safe. Or, at least, we thought we were.

I'm not too sure how long we'd been there, just our five families, surviving, living off what we could catch from the sea, but it seemed like forever, when they made contact over the VHF radio. We used the radios to talk to each other, to chat back and forth, and it was during one conversation that they broke in. They told us they were from the US Navy and that they'd been ordered to find as many survivors as they could and take them to a safe zone which had been set up in Puerto Rico. When they asked where we were, we gave them our position, and they told us they'd be there the following morning. That night, we celebrated. I felt as if a great weight had been lifted off my shoulders, and I slept soundly for the first time since *it* happened. Will didn't. He alone didn't trust the men who'd made contact with us. I never found out what it was, but there was something in the way they spoke that just didn't sit right with him.

I woke at daybreak to the sound of Will shouting angrily in the cockpit, followed by a blast from his shotgun. I leapt out of the bunk we shared and sprinted to the companion way. Will was standing on deck, gun pointed at someone I couldn't see.

'Get the fuck away from us!' Will yelled.

There was a shouted reply in what sounded like Spanish or Patois.

'Mom, what's going on?' Carol-Lynn had come up behind me and was now clinging to my side.

I smoothed her hair with my hand as I kept my eyes locked on Will. 'I don't know, honey.'

'Who's Dad shouting at?'

Before I could reply, Will fired the shotgun again. I'd always been against him having it on the boat; I thought it was too dangerous, especially with a child on board, but now I was glad we had it.

'Next time, I'll aim at your engine. You understand?'

Will's voice had a hard edge to it and they must have believed him, because I heard an outboard clunk into gear and race off.

He glanced down at me. 'Liz, we need to get out of here now. Get the engine started and as soon as I get the anchor out the sand, get us going.'

I looked at him questioningly. 'What's happening?'

'I'll fill you in later. There's not time now. They might decide to come back. They've gone over to the other boats, but they might still come back.' The hardness had gone from Will's voice and now he just sounded scared.

'Dad?'

'You stay down there, Carrie. It's not safe up here.' That's always what he called her: Carrie rather than Carol-Lynn. He was the only one who was allowed to call her anything other than her full name.

'But, Dad, what's going on?'

Will didn't answer. Instead, he disappeared towards the front of the boat. I leapt into the cockpit and started the engine. We hadn't used it in weeks, and it took several attempts before it spluttered into life. The shotgun lay on one side of the cockpit along with a pair of binoculars. While Will wrestled with the anchor line, I picked these up and scanned around the anchorage which had been our home for what seemed like a lifetime. There were three open boats, each about twenty feet long, fitted with large outboard engines, and twelve or thirteen men in all: some armed with machetes, others with clubs. One had what looked like an assault rifle, and two brandished pistols of some description. They'd boarded three of the other yachts already, and were circling the last one. Jools was standing on deck with his flare gun, doing his best to keep it pointed at which ever boat was nearest. Jenny was beside him and I figured their kids were probably somewhere down below. They'd overwintered at the same marina as us in Trinidad, and we'd got to know them well. I saw smoke rise from the barrel of the assault rifle just as the sound of the shot reached me and Jools crumpled to the deck clutching his arm.

'Liz, we need to get going now!' Will was striding towards the cockpit. I'd been so transfixed by what was going on with the other boats that I'd forgotten what I was meant to be doing.

'Oh ... yeah.' I lowered the binoculars and pushed the throttle forward, turning the wheel until we were heading out of the bay. We could only do about four knots at the most, and they'd easily be able to catch us if they wanted to, but it was our only hope of getting away. In the meantime, Will readied the sails.

The last I saw of the others was about fifteen minutes later. We were just about to round the top of the island where we'd pass from the attackers' sight. By then, they'd moved everyone onto the largest yacht and lined them up along one side; hands tied behind their backs, facing out to sea. While most of the strangers ransacked the other yachts, a group of three kept an eye on their prisoners. The one with the assault rifle leaned against the mast as he smoked a cigarette and chatted with the man sitting on the top of the cabin. The third walked back and forth behind our friends and their families, shouting and gesticulating with his pistol. I could see terrified looks on their faces.

'Mom, what's going to happen to them?' I hadn't heard Carol-Lynn come into the cockpit. She was standing beside me, her hand shading her eyes as she stared back towards the other boats. Her voice was quiet and flat.

I pulled her close. 'I don't know.'

'Can't we help them?' She was staring straight up at me.

I turned away, avoiding the blue eyes that were searching my face for answers. 'No.'

'Why not?'

Will looked across at her from where he was standing at the wheel, 'Because there's too many of them. They'd catch us too.'

'But what do they want?'

'Food, supplies, boats ...' Will caught himself just in time and glanced at me uneasily. He didn't finish his sentence but I knew what he'd almost said: *Women.*

Back on the largest yacht, I could make out Jools standing at one end of the line of people, Jenny beside him. Their kids, Michael and Jane, were there too. Jane was the same age as Carol-Lynn, and they'd spent a lot of time together since *it* happened. Michael was a couple of years younger. The man with the pistol was now behind Jools, still shouting and gesticulating. I saw Jools try to twist round to face him. He wasn't the type of person to just stand there and take it. The man pushed him back and then raised the pistol. I didn't hear anything, but as if in slow motion I saw Jools' head explode, and he toppled forward into the sea. Jenny tried to stop him, but with her hands tied there was nothing she could do. The man pressed his pistol against her head and, even though she was hunched over, she froze. The man shouted at her and she slowly straightened up. All the time the man kept his gun pressed against her. I could see him yelling at her; first in one ear, then the other. The one with the assault rifle was laughing.

After what seemed like an age, the man lowered the pistol and I saw Jenny relax a little. He took a step to his left and in a flash shot her two kids; not in the head, but in the back. Michael fell into the water where I saw him struggling to stay afloat, but Jane collapsed onto the deck. Jenny tried to get to her, but the man sitting on the cabin jumped to his feet and held her back. The one with the pistol stood over Jane and fired again and again into her belly. I saw her writhing in agony, while the man turned to Jenny and laughed. It was then that we passed round the headland and out of sight. That will always be my strongest, most lingering memory of the other families; the people we'd spent so much time with since *it* happened.

From then on, while we kept the VHF radio on, we swore we'd never use it. We kept mostly out at sea, well away from any land. It wasn't easy, but Will figured it was safer: there was less chance of us running into anyone else. We knew we needed others if we were going to survive, but we no longer knew if we could trust them.

It was late one night when I was on watch that I heard something coming over the airwaves. It wasn't clear, but it was definitely a voice.

'Help ... Please, help ... Someone, please help ... Help me.' It was a little girl, the fear clear in her voice. For a moment there was silence.

'I could go back in the head. I was in the toilet, reading ...' The signal faded out for a moment before coming back. '... blood everywhere.' Again, the voice was followed by silence. She was talking to someone I couldn't hear.

Suddenly, a new voice broke in; this time, a boy, a teenager by the sound of it. 'Katie, it's okay. Just do what Jack says. Get back in the head now.'

'Jeff, you're alive? Is everyone ...?' The signal disappeared, and they were gone. I listened on for the rest of my watch, but that was all I heard.

Over breakfast Will and I discussed it, trying to work out what it meant but before we could come to any conclusion the radio burst into life again.

'... Oh, hear us when we cry to Thee, for those in peril on the sea.' The voice was soft with a slight southern American accent.

It was an odd thing to suddenly hear. We both waited, but there was nothing more.

I glanced at Will, 'What d'you think that's all about?'

Will shrugged, 'Maybe it's Sunday and they're doing a service.'

I'd lost track of the days a long time before, and for all I knew it could be a Sunday. 'Where d'you think they are?'

Will scratched his head. 'Don't know. Maybe somewhere north of here. If they were further south we'd probably have heard them before now.'

'D'you think we should try to find them?'

'Don't know.' Will seemed to be saying that a lot these days. Over the years, I'd become used to him always having an answer, even if it was a guess, and this change was beginning to disturb me. It was almost as if he'd given up trying to make sense of the world.

'What about if we head north, see if we can pick up anything more?'

Will shrugged. 'I suppose.'

As we made our way north, the fragments of conversation coming over the radio gradually increased in frequency. We started to recognise voices and hear names: Jack, Rob, CJ, Jon, David. We got a sense of who they were and what they were doing: fishing, scavenging and, most importantly, surviving. It became addictive, and for a while, none of us spent more than a few minutes of our waking hours out of earshot of the radio, in case we missed something. Carol-Lynn was fascinated, and would make up stories based around what we heard, filling out the characters, giving them actions. CJ became a beautiful princess, trapped in a tower by Jack, her father. Rob, Jon and David were suitors she'd call down to, from a window high above the ground, sending them out on quests as trials, to see who would win her hand in marriage. Both Will and I laughed, but for all we knew she could have been right.

After a week, we heard a place name for the first time: Hope Town. Will scuttled below and returned with a chart. We spread it out and pored over it.

Carol-Lynn was the one who found it, perched on a small island around 100 miles to our north-west.

'What d'you think?' Will glanced at me nervously.

'It sounds like they're doing quite well; better than us at any rate. I mean you heard them talking about gardens and growing things the other day, didn't you?'

'Can we trust them though?'

'I don't know.' I was starting to use that phrase a lot too. 'It sounds like there're quite a lot of them though, like a proper community, not just a few people on boats. We could see if we could raise them on the radio. Find out more.'

'Yeah.' Will paused for a moment. 'But look what happened last time we made contact with anyone on the VHF.'

'This is different. We won't tell them where we are. There's no way they can work it out.'

'Still ...' Will's eyes flicked to Carol-Lynn. Like me, he was remembering the last we'd seen of her friend Jane, writhing in agony as a man tortured her in front of her mother; her father and her brother dead in the water.

'Yeah, maybe that's not a good idea.' I thought for a few seconds. 'How about if we head up there and see what we find? We can keep a low profile and if it looks dangerous, we can just creep away again.'

'Hummm ...'

I was starting to get exasperated. 'Will, we need to do something. We can't just float around out here for ever. Can we?'

'I suppose not.'
'So, we head up there?'
'Yeah, I guess.'

The first land we spotted was the southern tip of a large island called Great Abaco. We'd decided to work our way up along the coast towards Hope Town, to see what we could see. So far it was nothing, but then again the charts didn't show many settlements along the island's eastern coast at this end. As we moved north, I noticed the sea was beginning to change. The swell was gradually building into large, well-spaced rollers that would slowly lift the yacht up ten, fifteen feet and then drop it gently down again. Somewhere over the horizon a storm was brewing.

Later that afternoon, the VHF crackled into life yet again. It was doing this so often now we were starting to lose interest. Carol-Lynn had got bored with her stories and just made smart remarks about what the people were saying. She reckoned Jon fancied CJ, but didn't want anyone else to know. Who knew if she was right? Yet, there was one word in the latest fragment that instantly grabbed our attention. We recognised the voice from the accent even before he mentioned his name.

'Hey, this is Jack. We think there's a hurricane coming in. If you're not already in Hope Town, you need to come back here now ...'

Hurricane. That was the word which stood out, which frightened us. I didn't know how they knew one was coming, but it fitted with the building swell.

'Will, if there's a hurricane coming, we need to find some shelter.'

Will emerged from the companion way, waving a rolled-up chart. 'Way ahead of you.'

He laid it out in the cockpit and started glancing around. He pointed to an almost completely enclosed bay which housed a small settlement called Little Harbour. 'This looks good, and I think we can make it there before the storm gets here.' He glanced up at the sun. 'But I don't think we'll be there before it gets dark.' He inspected the chart more closely. 'We'll get as close as we can and then we'll just have to hope the storm doesn't get here before daybreak.'

By two in the morning, it was clear we wouldn't make it in before the storm got to us, and we had to decide what we'd do instead. The yacht was already starting to buck and sway in the ever-increasing seas. Working hard in the darkness, we stripped off the sails and the boom, so we'd have as little windage as possible. Will took an old storm jib and fashioned it into a sea anchor. As the winds built, he dropped it over the side and tied it off to the cleat on the foredeck. Almost immediately, the boat turned into the waves and started to settle. As I went down to get some rest, Will remained in the cockpit, bundled up in his oilskins and sou'wester against the rain, which was starting to move horizontally. At my insistence, he'd put on his life jacket and his safety harness. He sat there, staring out into the approaching storm, wondering, like I was, what was coming our way.

'Liz, we're in big trouble!'

Carol-Lynn and I had been jolted from the bunk where we were sleeping off the sea-sickness which had troubled us throughout the worst of the storm. Only in the evening when it started to ease did the queasiness begin to ebb away. We were both drained, physically and mentally, and had fallen asleep almost instantly. I glanced around, trying to get my bearings, and to work out how I'd ended up on the floor.

'Mom, I'm all wet.' Carol-Lynn had got up and was standing beside me, soaked to the skin.

Looking down at the floor I saw it was awash with water. I jumped to my feet. 'Will, what's going on?'

'We've hit something. Or rather, something's hit us.'

'What?' I was still trying to get my bearings.

'I don't know; something big in the water. It's put a hole in the side. We're going down.'

'Shit! What're we going to do?'

'I don't know. Get the dingy over the side, I guess. We'll have a better chance in it than in the life raft.'

'How long have we got?'

'Ten ... maybe fifteen minutes at the most.'

We got the dingy inflated and over the side in record time. I scrambled in, but just as Will was passing Carol-Lynn to me, the boat lurched onto its side and started to sink in earnest. A second later, it was gone, and Will was in the water. He grabbed onto the dingy and pulled himself over the side. He sat there, wringing wet and breathing heavily. After a second, he spoke. 'Fuck, that was close!'

'Dad, you're not meant to use words like that!'

I smiled. 'Darling, I think on occasions like this it's allowed.'

She looked confused as Will started the engine and turned us northwards. While the storm had eased, the waves were still high and towered above us whenever we sank into the troughs between them. It was slow-going, but at least we were heading in the right direction.

Then the engine spluttered and died, leaving us at the mercy of the sea.

'Will?'

He'd knelt down and unscrewed the cap of the fuel tank before peering in. He replaced the lid and stood up. 'Out of fuel.' He glanced around. 'We can't stay out here, not with the sea like this.'

'What can we do instead?'

'Paddle ashore?'

'But what about *them*?' We'd been at sea for so long, Will seemed to have forgotten about the danger which now lurked on land. 'What if there's infected there?'

'There's not many settlements around here, so maybe there won't be a lot around. If we find any when we get there, we can always head back out to sea.'

I pushed the wet hair out of my eyes. 'I suppose so.'

We untied the oars from where they were stored on the left side of the dingy, and taking one each, we started to make our way towards the nearby beach.

It took longer than I expected, and it was daylight before we finally climbed out onto the sand. It was the first time I'd set foot on land in months, and it felt strange, almost alien. I glanced around nervously, but there were no signs of life. To the south, sand stretched as far as I could see, while a rocky outcrop blocked our view to the north.

'Liz, help me get the dingy up the beach. I want to make sure it stays here in case we need it.'

'You have a plan then?'

'Yeah. See how far north we can get along the beach, and then see if we can reach any of the people in Hope Town on this.' He pulled out a small hand-held radio sealed inside a clear plastic bag from his pocket, and waved it from side to side.

'What will we do if we run into any of *them*?' Carol-Lynn always called the infected *them*, saying it in a slightly disgusted way. She couldn't bring herself to call them anything else. We'd seen what they could do when they attacked, not first-hand, but on the television when the news was still broadcasting. It had been horrifying to watch and Carol-Lynn still had nightmares about it.

Will reached into the dingy and pulled out a long thin package covered in plastic. 'Use this.'

He unwrapped it, revealing the shotgun. I was amazed he'd had the presence of mind to pack it as the boat was sinking. This was the Will I knew: the decisive decision-maker; the one I'd fallen in love with all those years ago. It was good to see him back. He'd been gone so long I'd wondered if I'd lost him forever. I hugged him; I couldn't help myself.

He looked at me, startled. 'What's that in aid of?'

'Just because.' I smiled, slightly embarrassed, and stepped away. 'Right, let's get going.'

He turned to Carol-Lynn. 'I almost forgot. I've got something for you.' She looked at him quizzically as he unzipped the front of his oilskin jacket and pulled something out. 'He's a bit wet, but I'm sure he'll recover.'

'Teddy!' She threw her arms around him. 'Thanks, Dad.'

We walked round it, examining it from all sides.

'Look, up there: blue and white paint. I think this is what we hit.'

The shipping container was nestled into the sand, twenty feet long, eight feet wide and a similar height.

Carol-Lynn was inspecting it curiously. 'What d'you think's inside?'

'I don't know, but it'd make a nice safe place to hole up.' Will banged the side and it echoed loudly. 'I don't think any infected could get into that!'

We set to work, clearing the sand away from the door. Once this was done, Will pulled up the lever and swung the door open. Inside was a jumble of cardboard boxes.

Carol-Lynn craned her neck. 'I wonder what's in them.'

'Only one way to find out.' Will reached for the nearest one and tore it open. Cans spilled out and rolled across the floor.

Carol-Lynn's eyes lit up with delight. 'Food!'

I picked up a can that had ended up against my foot, and held it out to her. 'I've never seen you get so excited over peas before.'

'Peas?' Carol-Lynn looked deflated. 'I thought it going to be something nice.'

It took us an hour to move enough boxes to allow us to enter the container. We stacked them along the back and sides until about half the floor area was cleared and we could move in.

I looked at Will. 'What now?'

'You guys stay here. I'm going to take a look around, and see if I can get an idea of what we're up against. Once I get back, we can work out what our options are.'

'Okay, but be careful.'

'When have I ever not been careful?' Will had a twinkle in his eyes, as he flicked them towards Carol-Lynn. It was a bit of an in-joke. We'd always talked about having kids at some point, but nonetheless, Carol-Lynn hadn't been planned. It wasn't that either of us regretted it, just that it had been a bit of a surprise when it happened.

Will hugged me, then Carol-Lynn. He took a few steps, then turned. 'Here, I should leave this with you.' He tossed me the plastic bag with the radio in it. 'Just in case.'

I stared at him, 'Just in case of what?'

He said nothing. Instead, he tucked the shotgun into the crook of his arm and strode off up the beach. I watched, not realising it was the last time I'd ever see him. Well, the *real* him anyway ...

'When's Dad coming back?'

It had been dark for an hour, and there was still no sign of Will. Just before sunset, I'd heard the sound of two shotgun blasts somewhere beyond the sand dunes at the back of the beach, and I'd expected him to come running over the top at any moment ... but he hadn't.

'He's probably been caught out by nightfall. He'll be holed up somewhere safe and sound. I'm sure he'll be back in the morning.'

'You promise?' Carol-Lynn glanced at me, but I couldn't bring myself to say anything. Of the two possible answers, one would be a lie, while the other would upset her greatly. Instead, I pulled her close and hugged her tightly.

By lunchtime, it was clear that Will was gone and I had to try and work out what to do next. I turned on the radio, and heard the people in Hope Town as they talked back and forth. I tried breaking in but it they were unable to hear me. If only I could reach them and let them know where we were, they might be able to come and get us. I tried to think of the reasons why I couldn't. I came to the conclusion it was one of two things: either the radio wasn't powerful enough; or there was something between us and them that was blocking the signal. There wasn't anything I could do to boost the power, but I could try and find a place where the signal would get through. I thought about how best to do this. The logical choice would be to go north, but that was where Will had gone and he'd obviously run into trouble. Then something occurred to me: what about the dingy? With just me and Carol-Lynn it would be difficult to paddle it any sort of distance, but we could tow it along behind us as we walked along the shore. This would give us a means of escape if we ran into trouble. I didn't know why this hadn't occurred to me before. If it had, Will might still have been with us.

I sat down beside Carol-Lynn on the boxes I'd arranged into a bed for her the night before. I held her hand. 'I think I've worked out a way for us to get out of here.'

'But we can't leave.' She had a shocked expression on her face. 'We need to be here when Dad gets back.'

I turned away, so she wouldn't see the tears welling up in my eyes. 'Dad's gone. He's not coming back.'

'He can't be.' Carol-Lynn was starting to cry now. 'He just can't be.'

'He is. And that means it's not safe to stay here. We need to get out, to get away before anything happens to us.'

'But ...'

'I know.' I held her tear-stained face in my hands. 'I know, but it's what we have to do. It's what Dad would have wanted us to do.' I kissed her on the forehead. 'The only thing is I'm going to have to leave you here for a little while. I need to go back to the dingy and bring it up here. Then we have to leave.'

'Can't I come with you?' She clung to me. 'I don't want to be alone.'

'No. You need to stay here in the container, where it's safe. If you come with me, I mightn't be able to protect you. I'd need to be able to run fast to get away, or jump in the water and swim. I can't do that if I'm worrying about you.'

'Don't leave me here on my own.' Her voice was quiet but plaintive. 'Please.'

'I have to,' I kissed her on the forehead again, 'It won't be for long, an hour at the most, but I have to. It's our best chance. I'll come back. I promise I will.'

I looked at the dingy. The tide was further out than when I was last here, and I knew it'd be a struggle to get it back into the water. As I stood there, trying to work out how I could do it, something hit me hard from behind throwing me forward onto the dingy. I twisted round to see Will standing over me, his eyes burning with anger. I'd never seen someone who was infected so close before, and the look of pure rage on his face chilled me to the bone. I could see a fresh wound on his forearm which still oozed blood. This must have been how he'd got the virus. For a moment he just stood there, staring: it was almost as if there was a hint of recognition. Then I realised he wasn't recognising me as me. Instead, he was seeing me as prey. I glanced down and saw one of the paddles to my right. As he lunged at me, I grabbed it and swung it at his head. Yet this was Will, the love of my life, and I only did it half-heartedly. He barely noticed and was on me in an instant. I felt an intense pain surge through my body as he sank his teeth deep into my left shoulder.

I still had the paddle in my hand and I raised it above my head. With all the force I could muster, I brought the blunt end down on the back of Will's skull. I did it again and again, until I felt it shatter. Even then I carried on, until I couldn't tell if he was moving because he was still alive, or because I was still hitting him. Finally, exhausted, I dropped the paddle and rolled him onto the sand. I sat there, staring at him disbelievingly. We had survived unscathed for so long, and now we were both finished. I could already feel the infection burning through my veins and I knew it was just a matter of time before it would overpower me. I wondered what I should do. I couldn't go back to the container, it would be too dangerous, but I didn't want to stay here with Will's body. Then it came to me. It was the last thing I could do for him, the man who'd been my best friend for most of my adult life, and it would take my mind off what was happening to me.

It took me an hour using the paddle to dig a hole in the sand that was big enough to bury Will in and it was another thirty minutes before he was covered up. By then I was sweating heavily, partly from the strenuous work but mostly because of the infection working its way through my body. I stood there, looking down. Unless someone told you, you'd never have guessed there was someone buried there beside the dingy. I said a small prayer for him before walking up to the top of the beach and sitting down. I surveyed my surroundings. It was the first time I'd really seen the place where we'd come ashore. With white sands, palm trees and blue seas, it was truly stunning. I couldn't imagine anywhere more beautiful to have buried the only man I'd ever really loved.

***

I can feel the end coming and my mind turns back to Carol-Lynn. I can't believe I'm leaving her alone on the beach. Her only hope now is that someone will find her. I know she's got plenty of food and I know there are other survivors around here, so I figure she's got a good chance just as long as she stays in the container. I turn on the radio just for some company before I go. There's a familiar voice, I think he's called Rob.

'Yeah Jack, I checked it out in the cruising guide. It looks small, but there might be something there. Andrew says it's a pretty easy trip.'

'I know the place.' It was the soft southern accent again. 'Just stick to checking out Little Harbour. Don't go any further south.'

My heart leaps into my mouth. It sounds like they're planning to come here ... and soon. I grab the radio, press the transmit button and shout as loud as I can, but I get no response. They just carry on with their conversation. I try again and again until I'm hoarse, doing do my best to let them know about Carol-Lynn, but still nothing. I look north towards the rocky outcrop which separates this part of the beach from the part with the container on it. I think about climbing to the top of it to see if it would make any difference, but if I do that, there's a risk I'll end up on the other side. I don't want that to happen. As long as I'm on this side and Carol-Lynn's on the other, I figure she's safer.

Rob's voice crackles out of the radio again. 'We'll leave in the morning, at first light, and should be there by noon. That way, we can be back well before nightfall.'

The words fill me with hope. They'll find Carol-Lynn tomorrow, I know they will. She won't be alone for long; just one night. If only I could tell her, but I can feel the virus taking over my body. I feel myself starting to fade; to disappear. Surely they'll see the container and investigate. How could they miss it? When they investigate, they'll find her. All she has to do is stay in the container and wait for them to get there. I've listened to them speaking to each other for days now. They sound like good people. I know they'll look after her. As the disease finally overcomes me, I smile to myself. I know that within a few hours my precious baby will be safe.

***

Author's Note: One of the most memorable scenes from *For Those In Peril On The Sea* is the one set in a container on the beach at Little Harbour. It's the one everyone talks about. My editor told me it haunted her for days after she read it for the first time. In the book, it's a bit of a mystery as to where the girl they find living in the container came from. I'd thought about writing her backstory into the book itself, but it didn't really fit in with the flow of the overall story, so I've written it here as a stand-alone piece. If you're familiar with the book you'll see where this dovetails into the main story. If not, you can read *For those in Peril on the Sea* to find out what happened to Carol-Lynn.

A Plague On Both Your Houses

Mercutio struggled to break into the crypt which held the bodies of Romeo and his young bride. The fighting between their two families had gone on too long and had cost too many lives, including his own. The need for revenge burned deep within Mercutio's body and it was this which had brought him back, when he should have remained still and lifeless in his grave. He knew he wasn't alive as such. Instead, he was little more than a walking corpse: he couldn't think clearly; he couldn't speak; but he could move; and what was left of his mind was consumed with an overwhelming desire to wreak revenge on those he blamed for his untimely death. With his dying words, Mercutio had sworn to bring a plague on both their houses, and now he was able to move again, he was going to make it happen. This wouldn't be a biblical plague of locusts or some creeping disease; instead, it would be a plague of his fellow dead. And at their head would be the two young lovers who'd died because their families bore a grudge for reasons none of them could even remember.

Having been dead for more than a week, Mercutio's muscles weren't as strong as they'd been in life, and he struggled to get into the crypt. Somehow he sensed that since he wasn't alive, he couldn't heal himself, and that if he damaged his gradually decaying body, he might not be able to satisfy the desire for revenge he felt burning through every fibre left of his being. He knew this meant he should be careful, but this hunger drove him onwards. Risking injury, Mercutio put his full weight to the door. With a sudden groan, he finally broke through and tumbled forward. Instinctively, he put out his arms to try to break his fall, snapping off two fingers as he hit the ground. Mercutio stared at them for a moment, watching as they skittered across the earthen floor and came to rest against the wall of the crypt. He wasn't alive, so it didn't hurt. Instead, it was just inconvenient. Leaving them where they lay, Mercutio pulled himself slowly to his feet and looked around. In the moonlight spilling through the broken door, he could see the bodies of the newly married bride and her secret groom lying next to each other. Soon, like Mercutio, they'd move again, and then he'd send them to do his bidding, bringing the same havoc to the lives of their warring families that they had brought to his. When he was finished with them, the Capulets and the Montagues would be no more, and Verona would be a better place for it. Then, and only then, would he let these star-crossed lovers rest, side by side, hand in hand, for all eternity.

***

Author's Note: Ever since *Pride and Prejudice and Zombies* was published in 2009, there has been a great interest in rewriting classics with a zombie twist. When I was looking around for a text on which to base my own literary zombie mash-up, I couldn't help but be attracted to *Romeo and Juliet*. It seemed to have everything on which a zombie story could be based: dead lovers; a grudge between two families; and even Mercutio's final words, wishing a plague on the two warring families, which forms the title of this piece. From that point onwards, the story pretty much wrote itself. While, at just under 500 words, this is a piece of flash fiction, I'm tempted by the potential to expand it into a full-length zombie sequel to the original play, which would tell the story of the revenge the dead Mercutio wreaks on the Montagues and the Capulets, with this short story acting as a prologue. This would be particularly poignant as he would not know that the deaths of Romeo and Juliet had finally reunited the two families and their feud was over. It might also be fun to introduce some characters from other Shakespeare plays into it, with the three witches from *Macbeth* being the obvious choice.

When Death Came To Flannan Isle

We sat round the wooden table as we did every day for lunch. It was the only time the three of us got to eat together, since one of us was always on duty at breakfast and supper.

'So, will this be your first Christmas on a rock then, Jim?' Murdo spoke in between mouthfuls of food. He always ate fast, shovelling in heaped spoonfuls, one after another. He'd barely have time to chew one before the next was on its way. It was disgusting to watch, but hypnotic too. It seemed impossible for anyone to eat that fast without choking, yet somehow he managed it.

'Aye, that it will.' While Jim was almost twenty-one, he still had the slender frame of a lanky teenager. He'd only been working the lights for a few months, and was still very much learning the lighthouse keepers' trade. He was just an occasional; someone sent to fill in whenever one of the permanent staff was needed elsewhere. Flannan Isle was his first deployment on a far-distant light: one that was little more than a cluster of whitewashed buildings, on a pinnacle of granite jutting out from a restless sea. It was only on the far-distant lights that you really felt the isolation. It could be weeks, sometimes months, before you got to speak to anyone other than your fellow keepers. All six of the tiny islands which surrounded the one with the light were uninhabited and, as far as I knew, they always had been. The nearest place with other people was Lewis, some twenty miles to the east. Given that we had no boat, it might as well have been on the far side of the moon, and anyway, it was hardly a great metropolis. For real civilisation you'd have to go more than 100 miles to Inverness, and that could take days.

'Well, we mightn't have much, and there's no drink, but we do alright, you'll see.'

I smiled across at Jim, 'Don't look so forlorn. A dry Christmas never killed anyone, and you'll be home by Hogmanay. I'm sure you'll more than make up for it then. 1900, the start of a new century; it's bound to be a night to remember. And I'm sure that not all the pretty girls in Aberdeen are taken.'

Murdo huffed. 'You ever been to Aberdeen? Ugliest women I've ever had the misfortune to meet.'

'Bet you didn't let that stop you though,' Jim shot back, without thinking. Once he realised what he'd said, he turned as white as a sheet. There's a very strict pecking order in lighthouses, and it wasn't an occasional's place to make fun of a head keeper, with twenty years' experience under his belt.

For the first time since I'd known him, Murdo's spoon stopped halfway to his mouth. At first, he had a look that seemed to be a mixture of surprise and anger, but after a few seconds, a broad grin spread across his weathered face. 'You're right there, laddie!' He emptied his spoon and carried on eating as fast as before, laughing to himself and shaking his head from side to side. 'You're right there.'

Not wanting to put his foot in his mouth again, Jim rose from the table and walked over to the window to check on the weather, while Murdo and I finished our lunch.

Jim had only been there for a few seconds when he cried out, 'Hey, there's a boat out there; not really a boat, more like a dingy.'

Murdo leapt to his feet, sending his chair crashing to the floor behind him. 'There's only one reason you'd get a dingy out here. Someone's in trouble. John, you come with me. Jim lad, you stay here.'

Murdo had worked on lights long enough to know it probably meant a ship had gone down, and that the sailors were making for the nearest land as it was their only hope of survival. Once we knew they were there, it was our duty to do all we could to help. At first, Jim seemed like he was about to protest, but he must have thought better of it, because he said nothing. Even though he was just an occasional, he knew the rules as well as the rest of us: no matter what happened, someone always had to stay in the light.

Murdo and I grabbed our oilskins and headed down to the east dock. As we did, we watched the small wooden boat grow slowly closer. The man at the oars looked spent, but somehow was still managing to power the boat towards the shore. Once on the dock, we could see he wasn't dressed for the sea. He was wearing what looked like an expensive tweed suit, as well as a collar and neck tie.

Murdo waved his arms over his head, 'Hey, you. Over here!'

The man didn't look round, but the direction of the boat shifted until it was heading straight towards where we stood. When the boat finally touched the shore, he collapsed across the oars.

'John, you stay here. I'll get him.'

Murdo moved with a speed that belied his size, and within a flash, he'd shimmied down the ladder leading to the water, and leapt into the wooden dingy. The first thing he did was tie it to the dock. Next, Murdo shook the man, but he didn't respond. Unperturbed, Murdo scooped him up and threw him over his shoulder before climbing back up to the dock. The man seemed lifeless, his head lolling back and forth with every step Murdo took.

Once they were on the quay, I could see the man properly for the first time. He was probably in his early thirties and had one of those thick moustaches, which seemed so fashionable these days amongst the middle classes. I glanced at his hands: while they were blistered and bleeding from rowing, I could tell they weren't the hands of a worker. His skin had the blue-grey tinge of someone who'd been out in the cold too long. I glanced at Murdo. 'We'd better get him inside as quick as we can; see if we can get him warmed up.'

'Warmed? What're you blethering on about man? He's burning up.'

I placed the back of my hand against his forehead and withdrew it immediately. He was so hot it was like touching a kettle that had just boiled on the stove.

**

'They're following me ... They're going to kill me ... Captain ... God ... Someone ... help me!'

We looked on helplessly as the stranger thrashed around in Jim's bunk. His skin was still tinged with grey but he was sweating so profusely that the sheets beneath him were sodden. While he'd not regained consciousness, he was murmuring deliriously, and although I couldn't make out all the words, I could tell he was petrified about something.

Jim scratched his head thoughtfully. 'He doesn't seem like a fisherman, or a sailor or anything, does he? How d'you think he got all the way out here?'

Murdo shot him a look that could curdle milk straight from the cow. 'Jim, that's none of our business.'

'But ...'

'Our duty is to care for him as best we can, not meddle in his private affairs. Whatever he's been through is between him and God.' Murdo paused for a moment. 'Or maybe him and the police.'

Suddenly, the man sat bolt upright and his eyes sprang open. For a second, he stared off into the distance. Then he started to scream. Before any of us could do anything he collapsed onto the bed, the sound of his cry still echoing around the small room.

Jim stared at him wide-eyed. 'I think he's dead.'

'Don't be daft, laddie. People don't just drop dead like that. John, check him.'

I leaned forward and placed my cheek over his mouth, but felt no breath; I put my hand on his chest, and felt no rise and fall; I held my ear against him, but there was no heartbeat. I straightened up again and glanced round. 'Jim's right. He's dead.'

***

'You don't think whatever killed him's infectious, do you?'

'If it is, me and Murdo are more at risk that you are. You never went near him, and we both touched him.'

'But he's in my bed. And on my sheets!'

Murdo put one of his massive hands on the boy's shoulder. 'Jim lad, we've got other things to worry about.'

'Like what?'

'Like what to do with his body. I mean, if we don't do something with it soon, it'll start rotting.'

If Jim had looked worried before, he looked worse now. 'Rotting?'

'Aye. When someone dies with a temperature like that, they'll start going off much sooner than usual.'

I scratched my beard as I tried to come up with a suggestion. We had nowhere to store a body, and the soil on the island wasn't deep enough to bury someone, so that option was out. It seemed there was only one answer left. 'It'll have to be a burial at sea.'

'Shouldn't we keep the body for the police to look at, or something?' Murdo and I turned to Jim.

'You've been reading that Sherlock Holmes rubbish again, haven't you, lad.' Murdo turned away, 'Bloody Conan Doyle, filling young boys' heads with his modern rubbish. There's no way we can tell anyone about this until the relief boat arrives on Boxing Day. He'll have rotted away to nothing by then. No, John's right. It'll have to be the sea for him.'

***

'Right, Jim lad, you grab his legs and I'll grab his shoulders.'

We were standing round Jim's bed, trying to avoid staring at the man's dead body. Murdo had laid some old sailcloth we'd scrounged up from the stores alongside him. As was traditional for a burial at sea, we were going to sew him into it, along with a few sizable rocks we'd gathered from the land which surrounded the lighthouse. They'd act as ballast, making sure he didn't float to the surface again, as he started to decay and bloat.

Jim grabbed the man's ankles and then let go almost immediately. 'Jings, he's still roasting hot!'

Murdo lent forward and slid his arms under the dead man's shoulders. 'It's just him starting to rot. Now, grab his legs.'

That was when the man moved. It was just a shiver, but it was definitely a movement. Jim and Murdo were too busy to notice it, but I did. Then his eyes flicked open. They were no longer blue. Instead, they were milky grey with dull black pupils: there was no doubt; these were the eyes of a dead man. He twitched again. This time Jim noticed too. He screamed and leapt away from the bed.

Murdo stayed where he was. 'What's gotten into you, laddie?'

Jim was now standing tight against the back wall, staring at the man. 'He ... he ... he ... he moved.'

'Don't be daft, Jim lad. Dead men don't move. It'll just be gas escaping or something like th—'

Murdo never got to finish what he was saying. The man's hands swung up, grabbing his hair and pulling him downwards. Murdo was caught unaware, and despite his size, he toppled forward. He screamed as the dead man sank his teeth deep into his neck, until blood spurted across the linen sheets and the whitewashed wall behind him. Murdo struggled, but the dead man had locked onto him and refused to let go. He bit Murdo again and again: on his throat, his face, his shoulders; any part he could reach. As more and more blood sprayed from his body Murdo started to weaken. Finally, he stopped moving and his body went limp. Still the dead man kept attacking, his teeth slicing into his flesh, his hands tearing at Murdo's now lifeless body.

'Jesus, John, is Murdo's dead? I think I'm going to ...' Jim made for the door but got only halfway before he threw up.

The sudden movement caught the dead man's attention and he seemed to notice Jim and me for the first time. He pushed Murdo's body to the floor where it landed in a crumpled heap. We watched, horrified, as he pulled himself to his feet and started to stumble towards us. His movements were stilted and sluggish as he lurched forward, Murdo's blood dripping from his mouth and face.

I swallowed hard. 'Jim, we've got to get out of here.'

Jim remained where he was.

I took a step forward and grabbed his arm. 'Jim, we need to get out of here now!'

That was all Jim needed to release him from the fear that was rooting him to the spot, and together, we turned and ran into the main room. Behind us, we heard slow, shuffling steps as the dead man started to follow.

'What're we going to do? That's a dead man back there and he's coming after us.'

'I don't know, Jim. Just let me think for a minute.'

'But he's coming ...'

Just then the dead man staggered into the room, letting out a low, visceral moan as he did so. I looked round for something I could use as a weapon. My eyes settled on the gaff hook we used to help land the fish we caught to liven up our otherwise dull diet. I grabbed it and swung it hard at the man's head. The sharp point pierced his skull just behind his left ear and sank so deep into his brain that the tip emerged from the centre of his forehead. Almost instantly, the man crumpled to the ground, pulling the makeshift weapon from my hand. I'd have said he died if he hadn't been dead already, but something, some life force, certainly left him.

Still, neither Jim or I was keen to approach. We'd seen what had happened to Murdo when he'd been caught by surprise, and we didn't want the same to happen to us. Minutes passed without any movement, and I finally decided it was safe. I knelt down next to the stranger's body and examined it. His shirt had come loose and I could see what looked like a bite mark on his side. It was deep enough to have drawn blood, and while it looked a couple of days old, there was no sign it had started to heal. Instead, it remained a festering wound that oozed a thick, black liquid.

To my right, Jim let out a startled yelp, followed by a scream so filled with pain it could only have been made by a dying man. I leapt to my feet and spun round to find Murdo standing behind Jim, his massive arms wrapped round him, his teeth buried deep into the side of his head. Jim tried feebly to fight, but the damage was too much. After a second, he went limp and Murdo let go of his body. As it fell to the ground, Murdo turned towards me. His eyes were clouded and lifeless; his skin as grey as the granite beneath our feet. Blood oozed from the bites which covered his head and neck as he lurched forward, arms reaching out towards me, hands grasping the air. I tried to free the gaff hook, but it was too firmly embedded in the dead man's skull. Realising that Murdo would be on me in seconds, I left it there and ran for the stairs which led up to the top of the lighthouse.

***

I've been hiding in the light for five minutes now. I can hear Murdo slowly but inevitably getting closer and closer. There's 185 steps between the bottom and the top of the tower, and I've listened to Murdo clamber up every single one of them. He's moving unsteadily, bumping off the walls, stumbling here and there, but then again he's dead, so I have to give him credit for still being able to get up the stairs at all. It's given me time to make a plan though, and I'm ready for him when he finally steps into the light. It's only three o'clock in the afternoon, but the darkness is starting to grow outside and I should be getting the light ready to send its signal out into the night. Instead, I'm preparing to kill Murdo ... Or whatever it is I need to do to stay alive. After what he did to Jim, I'm under no illusions as to what he'll do to me if I let him get his hands on me. I've known Murdo for eleven years, but I'm not going to let him do that to me; not over my dead body ... or his.

As Murdo lumbers closer, I back off towards the door to the balcony, which surrounds the outside of the light. In my hand, I'm grasping the leg of a chair I'd broken into pieces so I'd have some sort of weapon to defend myself. I step out into the sea air and wait for Murdo to follow. Like a bloodhound, he tracks my every movement. Even though his dead eyes don't see any more, he knows where I am. Maybe he hears me or smells me, or something, but however he's doing it, he definitely knows where I am. I wait for him to step through the door. The change in temperature seems to disorient him for a second or maybe it's the wind that's starting to whip around the light as the sun goes down. I take my chance and smash the chair leg into his skull sending him spinning towards the guard rail. I hit him again and again, but he won't go down. Finally, I pull back and swing as hard as I can. I catch him across the side of the head and send him over the edge. Unfortunately, I swing with such force that the chair leg slips from my grasp and spins off into the gloaming, but it doesn't matter; Murdo is already falling the seventy-five feet to the ground. Even dead, there's no way he's surviving that sort of fall.

I'm peering over the rail looking at Murdo's shattered body just to make sure he's properly dead when I feel the bite on the back of my neck. I spin round to find Jim standing behind me, my blood dripping from his open mouth. Without thinking, I grab his shirt and throw him over the guard rail. He's so slight that it's not difficult for someone like me. I don't like doing it, but I can tell from his eyes that he's dead already; he just doesn't seem to know it yet. I'm guessing he will when he hits the ground. I slump onto the deck of the balcony knowing that all of this is finally over, and wondering how I'm going to explain it to the lighthouse board, but after a couple of minutes, I notice something. There's a heat radiating out from where Jim just bitten me; I can feel it spreading throughout my body. That's when I finally put two and two together. The dead man had been bitten by someone; he bit Murdo; Murdo bit Jim; and Jim bit me. Whatever it was that killed him while making him walk again, it was infectious … and now I have it.

I leap to my feet, not knowing how long I have, but I have to do something to break the cycle of infection. None of these bodies can be here when the relief ship arrives, and neither can I.

***

It had taken all my strength to load the three bodies into the dingy and row it out to where I knew the water was more than sixty fathoms deep. It seemed only fitting that whatever the disease was it was leaving Flannan Isle the same way it arrived.

One by one, I heave the bodies over the side, knowing they'll never surface again, not all the way out here. I say a prayer for each of them in turn. I've cleaned everything up at the lighthouse so no one will ever be able to work out what happened; it's better that our families don't know. After all the exertion, I'm exhausted and I sink down into the bottom of the dingy. It's now dark and I can make out the stars above me in amongst the clouds. I can feel the movement of the small boat as it's lifted up and down by the swell passing underneath me. I no longer have the strength to do what I intended; to throw myself over the side with my pockets filled with rocks. I can feel the infection, whatever it is, burning through my veins. It's only a matter of time before it kills me and then I don't know what will happen. I stare up at the sky. I can see the constellation of Orion just above the left-hand side of the boat. I try to get up, but I no longer have the strength. All I can do is lie here, hoping that it won't hurt as badly as it seemed to hurt the dying man we'd rescued from the dingy less than half a day before.

The new century is only a few days away, but I know I'll never see it dawn.

***

Author's Note: The lighthouse on Flannan Isle is a real place off the west coast of Scotland (follow this link to see its location in Google Earth: http://www.forthoseinperil.net/_files/Flannan_Isles_ Lighthouse.kmz – this requires that you have either Google Earth or the Google Earth Mobile app installed on your computer), and this story was inspired by a real event which took place there in 1900. It has entered Scottish mythology, and in many ways, it is our *Marie Celeste* or our *Bermuda Triangle*. I touched on it towards the start of *For those in Peril on the Sea,* where one of the characters is reminded of the memorable line 'Three men alive on Flannan Isle who think on three men dead', from the poem by Wilfrid Wilson Gibson, about Flannan Isle.

The basic summary of the story is this: On Boxing Day (as the day after Christmas is known in Britain) of that year, a relief ship arrived to find the lighthouse deserted. Some say there was food left untouched on the table and no signs of a struggle, although this part may well be fiction. No trace was ever found of the three lighthouse keepers who should have been manning the light, and to this day, no one really knows what happened to them. To all intents and purposes they just disappeared into thin air. For more information about this mystery, visit http://en.wikipedia.org/ wiki/Flannan_Isles.

I'm in no way implying that this is what happened and, out of respect, I have specifically chosen not to use the real lighthouse keepers' names for the characters in this story. In addition, I've set it in the preceding year (1899), rather than

1900. Without any modern technology, this would have been a time when the men keeping a far-distant light such as Flannan Isle would have been cut off from the rest of the world for much of the time, and this adds to the tension within the story since the lighthouse keepers know there's no way they can call for help from the outside world. It's just them against whatever's happening on the island.

Family

I hear my dad stumble through the front door and collide with the coffee table, sending empty wine bottles skittering across the floor. He's drunk again, but for once, he doesn't swear. I know what's coming next: the argument with my stepmom, the fighting — she drinks in the house while he goes to his usual sports bar — followed by my little sister crawling into my bed so she feels safe. If it hadn't been for her I'd have runaway years ago, but I stay to protect her until she's old enough to come with me. I fold my pillow over my ears, trying to enjoy the last few seconds of calm before the inevitable storm, which happens around this time almost every night. Tonight it doesn't; there's no yelling, no sound of my dad lashing out. I'm just beginning to wonder what's going on when the silence is shattered by an ear-piercing scream. I know from the pitch it's my sister, Sally, and I leap from my bed, grabbing the baseball bat I've kept behind my bedroom door ever since the night my dad slapped me around. As I'd nursed my split lip and black eye, I'd decided I was never going to let him hit me again without giving him back a lot worse than I got. That was five years ago, and he'd yet to try it again. I think he could see from the way I looked at him that it wasn't worth the trouble, not when there were others he could take it out on, who he knew wouldn't fight back.

I enter the narrow corridor linking all the rooms in our apartment and find Sally standing at the entrance to my dad's bedroom staring open-mouthed. She must have been on her way to my room when something stopped her in her tracks. My stepmom had passed out on the sofa at nine, and as usual, we'd carried her through and dumped her on their bed, so I can't understand what Sally's so transfixed by. There are noises coming from the room, but they don't sound like anything I've heard before. I tiptoe over to Sally, the baseball bat loosely held in my right hand, put my arm around her to try to steer her away and glance into the room. Instantly I freeze. My dad's on top of my stepmom, biting at her neck, tearing at her with his teeth. Blood's spraying all across the white sheets and the magnolia walls, and for some reason, the first thought that enters my head is that she'll be real mad when she sees the mess. Then I think, *this is bad, even for him.* Sally whimpers as I draw her to me, and this seems to get my dad's attention. He stops gnawing on my stepmom and turns to face us. That's when I see his eyes for the first time. They're burning with something I've never seen before, not even when he's at his worst. A second later, he's on his feet and racing towards us. I don't think, I just take a step forward and swing the bat. I feel it connect with his head and even though he's my dad, it feels good. Everything I've been bottling up since my mother died, and I realised what a mean drunk my father really was, comes bubbling to the surface: the time he beat my stepmom so badly she couldn't get out of bed for three days; the fact I feel trapped in my own personal hell, unable to grow as a person, to become the adult I so much want to be, while I'm still under the same roof as him. I put all of it into swinging the bat again and again, until he stops moving. Only then do I realise what I've done.

He lies motionless on the floor, half in the bedroom, half out of it. I glance from his body to that of my stepmom. She's pale and still, and I know she's dead. Suddenly, her arm trembles. Maybe it's more of a twitch, but it's definitely movement. Given how much blood she's lost, I know she can't still be alive, but she's moving. I crouch down and examine my dad's lifeless body. His eyes are open and I can see the whites are a deep red; not the bloodshot red of when he was drunk or hung-over but something altogether different. Hesitantly, I reach out and touch him, then quickly draw back in surprise: his skin's cold; not just cool, but as cold as ice. Then my stepmom sits up and slowly turns towards us. That's when I grab Sally's hand and run.

I don't know where we're going. I just know we need to get out of here. I race down the stairs of our apartment building and within seconds, we're out on the street. It's dark, but all around us I can see shadows moving. My brain's spinning, trying to process what I've just done; trying to work out what's going on all around me. Then I realise Sally's crying. I crouch down so I can look her in the eye, 'Look, I don't know what's happening, but no matter what, I'll keep you safe,' I tell her. 'I promise.' I try to pull her towards me, to hug her, but she resists.

She sniffs and wipes her eyes with the sleeve of her pyjamas, 'You killed Dad!'

'I had no choice. You saw what he did to her. He'd have done the same to us.'

'But you killed him!'

I understand why Sally's upset; she loves him and she's too young to really realise what a drunk he is, or rather was, and how crappy this made our lives. It's partly my fault; I tried to keep as much of it from her as I could, and made sure that he never hit her the way he hit Macy; that's my stepmom's name. Well, that was her name. Suddenly, Sally's eyes widen as she stares at something over my left shoulder, and she screams again. I hear a noise behind me, a sort of low guttural groan and spin round to find Macy staggering towards us. The gaping wound on her neck is dripping blood onto her pink nightdress, and her eyes now look red and empty like my dad's. Still not quite knowing what's happening, I pull Sally behind me and lift the baseball bat. Macy's eyes seem to stare straight through me and her head lolls slightly to one side, but she seems to know we're there because she's moving faster now. I wait until she's within reach and swing the bat. She goes down, and instantly, I feel sorry. She wasn't a bad person, not really. She'd just made some poor choices in life: the main one being marrying my dad. I don't think he even told her he had two kids before she moved in and found us there, but she always did her best. It's just that her best wasn't much good.

A movement catches my eye and my head whips round. There, shuffling out of the darkness and into the pool of light cast by the nearest street lamp, are three people. I stare at them in disbelief: one has half his face missing, and the other two have bloodstains on their clothes and around their mouths. Like Macy, they're lurching towards us, arms outstretched, quickening their pace with every step. I glance round and see another two coming from the opposite direction. I know we'll soon be surrounded, but I can't see a way to escape. All I can do is try to keep Sally behind me and raise the bat in readiness. Just before I can take my first swing there's a squeal of tyres and the people staggering towards us are gone, replaced by a black car. Not needing to be asked twice, I pull the back door open and push Sally in, before throwing myself after her. Almost as soon as my feet leave the ground I feel the car accelerating away. It swings to the left and there's a dull thud as it hits something before bumping over it. I call out to the driver as I struggle to sit up and strap Sally in, 'D'you know what's going on?'

'Zombies!'

'What d'you mean zombies?'

'You know,' he looks at me for a second, but I'm busy trying to deal with Sally, 'The dead come back to life, walkers, flesh-eaters ...' There's something familiar about his voice, but I can't quite put my finger on what.

I interrupt him. 'But zombies don't exist!'

'They mightn't have done before, but they sure do now. I don't know why, but they're everywhere. That's why I'm getting out of here.'

Only then do I get a chance to check the driver out properly, and my heart drops.

I stare at the back of his head. 'You!'

He glances in the rear-view mirror. 'Yeah, me.'

There's an awkward silence. I've known Nick since before I can remember. When we were little we played together all the time because his mom was friends with mine, but she stopped coming around after Mom died. I still saw Nick at school, but as we'd grown up, we'd grown apart. I'd been so embarrassed when last year, completely out of the blue, he'd asked me to the prom. I don't know what possessed him, because I'd worked so hard to become one of the cool kids and he'd grown up to be a geek, so he must have known there was no way I could possibly go with him. I'd felt so sorry for him when he'd had to slink away back to his locker as my friends sniggered, but there was nothing I could do about it.

Now, sitting there behind him in his car after he'd just saved my life, I figure I should say something. 'I could have handled them myself, you know.' I can't work out why I said that; it's so *not* true, and we both know it.

Nick smiles at me, a sad look in his eyes. 'You don't have to do everything yourself, you know. You're allowed to let other people help you.'

I get the feeling he's not just talking about tonight, and I look at him curiously.

He keeps his eyes on the road as he carries on, 'I know about your dad. I've known for years, even before that night. I heard my mom talking about him, but no matter what I tried, you never let me help you.'

That's when I remember something I haven't thought about in years. The night my dad hit me, I'd run away and it was Nick's house I'd run to. I'd knocked on his bedroom window and he'd let me in. I didn't tell him what had happened, but he could see the state I was in. He cleaned me up and then just hugged me as I cried. When I woke in the morning I felt embarrassed, both about what my dad had done and about the fact that I'd fallen asleep in Nick's arms. I'd snuck out and walked home, because I didn't know where else to go. My dad was still asleep, passed out on the sofa in the living room. I found Sally curled up in my bed; the only one in the house who'd even realised I'd been gone all night. After that, I'd never felt comfortable with Nick again. Outside of my family, he was the only one who was aware of what my dad was really like, and I couldn't bear to be around someone who knew my darkest secret.

Trying not to blush at the memory, I glance out the window.

'You want me to drop you off somewhere, or you want to come with me?' I turn to find Nick looking at me expectantly.

I think about this for a moment. I've got friends, lots of them, but none of them are real friends. If any of them ever found out what my life was really like at home, none of them would speak to me again. They'd think I was too weird, too abnormal; they wouldn't realise I was the same person they'd always known. It's so unfair, It's not my fault my dad was a vicious drunk; I didn't choose him. That's when I realise that ever since my mom died I've felt alone. I've pushed away anyone who really cared about me, I've put up barriers, and specifically chosen to hang out with people who are so shallow they wouldn't notice that I never asked them round to my house, or that I had to look after

Sally all the time. Then I realise Nick knows about me — the real me — about how screwed up my life is. He knows all this and he still likes me. This gives me a warm feeling inside.

I glance at him, noticing for the first time that he's not bad looking really. 'Where you heading?'

'My uncle's place. He's got a farm out in the country. He's got guns and stuff there.' He flicks the steering wheel to the right, and ploughs through a pair of zombies that are shambling down the middle of the road. 'I figure it's as safe as anywhere is now.'

I've never been out of the city before, or at least not as far as I can remember. There are some memories with my mom that might have been on a beach, but I can never see them clearly: there're too many others in the way, bad ones. For some reason, the thought of leaving the city excites me. I guess it's because I've wanted to leave for so long and now it's actually happening.

Nick slams on the brakes, 'Oh, ffff—' He glances at Sally and stops himself. 'Flip!'

Ahead there's a solid mass of people all shuffling towards us. Even over the sound of the engine I can hear them moaning and groaning. Sally clings to me, terrified by the sight, and starts to cry again.

I look at Nick, 'What're you going to do?'

'I don't know. Let me think for a minute.'

'I know, take a left up that alley there.' Whenever my dad drove drunk — and that was a lot — he always kept off the main streets, choosing the back alleys instead. He said it was because they were safer, but as I got older I realised it was so that he didn't get stopped by the cops. On the plus side, it means I know them better than the back of my own hand, and I know the one up ahead will take us safely round the people — or rather zombies — that are blocking the street. Without questioning it, Nick does as I tell him. I guide him between the tall tenement buildings and back onto the street about a mile further on. As we rejoin it, I twist round and stare in the direction we just came. I can see the mass of zombies off in the distance, still staggering forwards, and I know we're clear of them.

***

We're out of the city now and the car's racing through the night. Despite everything, Sally's fallen asleep in the back seat, and I've climbed into the front alongside Nick. We haven't seen a zombie since the suburbs. In fact, we haven't seen anyone else on the road. It's like the three of us are the only people left in the world. Nick's got a CD on, something quiet and mellow I haven't heard before, and I've got the passenger window open: I'm playing with the air that's streaming past. It smells different from city air: cleaner, almost crisp. All around us there's darkness, while above our heads are stars, millions of them. I can't believe how many there are. I've always known they were up there, but I've never seen so many before because of all the lights in the city. Nick sees me staring up at them and grins. He seems to know what's going through my head and he starts telling me about them. 'See those ones there? They make up a constellation called Orion, and the ones over there that look like the letter W, that's Cassiopeia.'

'Cassiopeia?' I know the name from somewhere but I can't quite place it.

'Yeah, she was an ancient Greek queen who boasted about how pretty she was and the gods punished her by making her sacrifice her daughter, Andromeda, to a sea monster, but Perseus saved her because he was in love with her. They're up there too. That's Perseus over there, and that's Andromeda there.'

I try to follow where he's pointing. I can't make out which stars he's talking about, but for some reason it's nice to know they are up there, immortalised forever. Nick doesn't seem to notice that I don't know which stars he's talking about.

'See that bright star there in the middle of Andromeda? It's ninety-seven light years away. That means the light we're seeing now left there at the start of the last century.' He glances at me as if trying to judge what I'm thinking. He must be able to see I'm interested because he carries on. 'But that's nothing. See that star there? That's Deneb. It takes the light from it more than 1,000 years to get here. The light we're seeing left there more than 500 years before Columbus discovered America. Then there's ...'

'Nick,' I interrupt, 'where'd you learn all that stuff?'

'Don't know. I just sort of picked it up. I find it interesting. I guess my dad told me a lot of it, and the rest I got from books.'

I thought about this for a few seconds. All my dad had ever taught me was never to wake him when he had a hangover, and to keep out of his way when he was drunk. At that moment, I feel both angry and sad, and then for some reason I miss him, and I start to cry.

Nick puts his hand on my shoulder, just for a second, to let me know he understands, and then puts it back on the wheel. I pull myself together and wipe away the tears before clearing my throat. 'So where d'you think the zombies came from?'

He looks at me, 'I don't know. I was out on the roof trying to see the meteor shower, and I saw Mr Lafferty from next door staggering up the street, only he died last week. I know because Mom went to his funeral on Monday. I went inside and told her, but she wouldn't believe me. I wish she had because the next thing I know Mr Lafferty crashed through the front door and grabbed her by the hair and sank his teeth into the back of her neck. It was horrible: there was blood everywhere and she was screaming like I've never heard anyone scream before. Dad tried to stop him, but he couldn't. I wanted to stay and help, but Dad told me to take the car and go. I think that's the only reason I got out alive. The last thing I saw was Dad hitting Mr Lafferty over the head with a frying pan, but he was bleeding a lot and I could tell he wasn't going to survive for long.'

There's sadness in his voice, and I think about what he's just said. That's the difference between our dads: when the dead started walking, his saved his life; mine tried to kill me. It takes me a second to realise there are tears running down Nick's face. Knowing he'll be embarrassed if I mention it, I stare out the window for a couple of minutes. When I turn back to him, the tears are gone, but his eyes are still red. 'How long will it be till we get to the farm?'

'About an hour.' His voice breaks, and he tries to cover it up by clearing his throat.

'You think we'll be safe there?'

'We should be. It's in the middle of nowhere. There's no one around for miles.'

'What about your uncle?'

He shifts uncomfortably in the driver's seat 'He's ... errr ... away on business.'

I figure that's a lie, but I don't push him further on it. Instead, I ask another question, one that's been eating away at me ever since it first popped into my head. 'Nick,' I hesitate for a moment, 'do you think everyone who's dead has come back? Or only some of them?'

He seems to know what I'm thinking and avoids looking at me. 'I don't know, but it's probably only people who've died recently. None of the ones I've seen were rotting or anything like that. They all seemed — you know — fresh.'

Despite its gruesomeness that makes me happy. I don't want my mom to have come back as one of them.

I turn towards Nick, 'But what about my dad?'

'What d'you mean?'

'When my dad came home tonight, he was one of them. He killed my stepmom and he tried to attack us. I had to bash his head in with that just to stop him.' I point to the baseball bat in the back seat. It seems weird to be telling someone what I did, but I know Nick will understand. 'He didn't die, or at least I don't think he did. How did he become one of them?'

'I guess he must have been attacked and got bitten. I think it might have started with dead people, but when they bite live people, I think they infect them with something, and then they turn into zombies too.'

That certainly explained what went on with my stepmom.

I think about all that's happened in the last few hours, and try to work out how I'm feeling. As I'm figuring it out something odd strikes me. The dead might have risen and taken over the world, but I've finally got the escape I've dreamed of for years. It doesn't matter that my dad and my stepmom are dead, or that they tried to kill me. What matters is that I've finally broken free. I know life isn't going to be easy now the world's changed, but I've survived this long and now I've got out, I know I can keep going, no matter what.

I glance first at Nick and then at Sally. They are my family now, and despite all that's happened, I'm happier than I've been for a very long time. It might have taken the world coming to an end, but finally I realise that your family doesn't have to be the one you were born into: it can also be the people you choose it to be.

***

Author's Note: This story was written as a brief venture into the rapidly expanding and ever-popular 'Young Adult' or 'YA' genre: that is, one aimed at a teenage audience, so it couldn't be as grim and gruesome as some of the other zombie stories in this book, and it had to explore themes which would both appeal and be familiar to younger readers.

I chose the theme of a dysfunctional family, because I think this is something many teenagers can relate to. I also wanted to explore the rather depressing fact that, for some young people, a zombie apocalypse, bad as it would be, could actually improve their lives rather than make it worse. In this case, it gives the girl telling the story the chance to escape from her drunken and violent father. Who knows if her life will be better in the long term, but for the moment, for the first time in her life, she feels free.

Three Men In A Boat

There're three of us crammed into a row boat built for two, floating in the middle of the millpond. It seemed like such a good idea when we scrambled into it to escape the horde of undead that descended on our village without warning, but now we realise it was the wrong thing to do. We can see the zombies crowding the nearby shores, moaning and shuffling, surrounding us on all sides. They know we're here; they can sense us; but they can't get to us, so it seems like we're safe. Yet, there's no way we can escape either, and we don't have anything we can eat. All we can do is huddle together, making sure the dingy doesn't drift too close to the shore, and hope that somehow, someone comes and rescues us.

The Emergency Room

I regain consciousness to find I'm strapped to a bed and cannot move. I hear someone shuffling towards me and see a flash of white coat. There's an odd odour in the air, almost like decaying flesh. A shadow looms over me, then teeth tear into my neck and I know I'm going to die.

Survival Skills

Something's wrong. I can't put my finger on what yet, but I've always been able to sense when things are amiss. It's what has kept me alive since the dead unexpectedly and inexplicably rose from their graves. Some saw this as a sign of *The Second Coming*, and ran forward, arms open in greeting. No sooner had this welcoming committee reached the no-longer-quite-so-deceased than they were devoured. The dead might be dead, but it hadn't dented their appetite, and it seemed that, above all, they craved human flesh. Maybe they just wanted what they no longer had: blood coursing their through veins; a still-beating heart; a brain sizzling with electricity. Once the true believers had been consumed, the dead turned their attention to the rest of us: chasing us down, pursuing us like prey. They might stagger and stumble, but they're relentless; grinding down your resistance day after day after day.

When it started, the army were sent in to stop them, but soldiers are trained to kill, and they didn't know quite what to do when faced with an enemy that was dead already. That is not to say they didn't try; they did. It's just they didn't do much good. After that, it was every man for himself — or, in my case, every woman.

Suddenly I realise what's wrong: the birds have stopped singing and the forest around me has fallen silent. That, I've learned, is a sure sign the dead are approaching. I freeze, listening, trying to work out where they are and how I can escape one more time. I don't really know what I'm doing but I must be doing something right. After all, I may well be the only one still breathing in this world where the dead now stalk the living.

***

Author's Note: This story started off as a challenge to write a complete story in 300 words and it comes in at 297, so that target was reached. However, despite its short length, it still explores a number of themes, including whether some religious groups would see a zombie apocalypse as a sign of *The Second Coming of Christ*; the fact that soldiers may well have a hard time fighting zombies, because they'd be facing a type of enemy they've never faced before, and one against which their usual tactics are unlikely to work; and also that to survive in a world filled with zombies will be a constant struggle, and you'll have always be on guard.

The Custom Of The Sea

16th May: This is the twentieth day since the dead came back to life. Well, not really life, but a pale imitation of it, which comes with an insatiable hunger for human flesh. I don't know why I've decided to start keeping a diary now, but I have. I think it's to do with Martin's death. He died this morning; probably from starvation. We're all pretty close, but he was the first to go, and now there's only seven of us. I always hated this place, yet now it looks like I'll spend what little is left of my miserable life here, with the colleagues I despise so much. Martin was the only one I liked. Now he's gone, I feel lonely and abandoned. I knew we should have run right at the beginning, when we still had the chance, but the others persuaded me it would be better to pull down the shutters, lock ourselves in, and wait for the authorities to deal with the dead that were wandering the streets and attacking the living. Within a day, it was clear there were too many of them for the army or anyone else to deal with, but by then, we were trapped, just the eight of us, in the warehouse. We'd be okay if the company we worked for sold food, but it didn't; it sold stationery. We've tried going outside to search for supplies but the dead are everywhere, and they always chase us back in before we get more than a few feet. We've seen from the upper windows what happens when the dead catch the living; it's not pretty, and none of us want to go that way, but still, we need to find something to eat or, like Martin, we'll starve to death, and there's nothing to eat in here.

17th May: I woke this morning to find the others discussing what to do with Martin's body. We kept away from it at first, frightened he might come back, but he didn't. He just lay there, eyes sunken, cheeks hollow, his arms as thin as sticks. Steve was talking about starting a fire, and initially, I thought he was suggesting we cremate Martin. Then I realised Steve was talking about cooking and eating him. The very thought of doing that makes my stomach churn with disgust, and I can't believe he'd even suggested doing something so awful. Surely he can't be serious?

18th May: For the first time since it happened I have a full belly, but it makes me feel sick to think of what I've done. Steve was the one who did it; who cut Martin up into thin slices with a box cutter and cooked him on a fire he made from the reams of A4 paper that surrounded us. At first, I didn't want to eat, but the smell of the cooking meat was too tantalising: it smelled just like bacon and my body couldn't resist. It wasn't like we killed him, and I'm sure Martin would have wanted us to do all we could to survive.

25th May: We ate the last of Martin four days ago, and we're starting to get hungry again. Steve keeps going on about something he calls 'The Custom of the Sea'. He says it's an unspoken rule for people who find themselves trapped like us. He says it's better for one of us to die so that the others can live long enough to be rescued, than for all of us to die. I don't know exactly what he's talking about, but I don't like the sound of it.

26th May: Steve has finally made it clear what 'The Custom of the Sea' is. He wants us to draw lots. Whoever picks the short straw would then kill themselves, so that the rest of us could eat. Thankfully, no one seems keen on the idea.

28th May: We drew lots today, and it was Jimmy who lost. He looked dumbfounded at first, then he started shouting that he wasn't going to do it. Steve said that was okay, that it had to be voluntary, but that we'd all agreed to the rules before we'd drawn lots, and that he had a moral obligation to honour his word. Jimmy just refused.

29th May: I woke this morning to find Jimmy was dead. Steve told me he'd seen reason and had slit his throat in the bathroom, but something seems wrong there. Jimmy was so against the idea last night, and I can't see what would have changed his mind. I was going to say something, but before I could, the smell of cooking flesh started to swirl around me. It made my mouth water and all I could think about was how great it will taste. When it was ready, I ate as greedily as the rest of them, but afterwards, when I had time to think about what I'd just done, I almost threw up. Somehow I managed to keep it down though. Later, I went upstairs and looked out of the window. The dead are everywhere: stumbling and shuffling around. I think they must know we're in here, because they're crowding tightly around the shuttered doors now, trying to force their way in. I was hoping I could see a way out, but I can't; there's just too many of them. I went into the office where I used to work; the one administrator overseeing those on the warehouse floor. The phone lines are still down, and with no power I can't turn on the TV. I did find an old battery-powered radio, but all I could find on it was static. It's like we're the only people left in the world. In a sudden and all-consuming fit of frustration and rage at what I'd been reduced to, I picked up my chair and smashed it repeatedly against the wall. It didn't do anything to change our situation, but as I surveyed the broken pieces of wood scattered across the floor, I felt better for it.

3rd June: Steve's talking about drawing lots again, but this time he says we have to draw twice: once to see who we'll eat; and once to see who'll kill them. He says this is so that the person can't back out like Jimmy did. This confuses me because I thought Jimmy killed himself. Then I realise he didn't, and that Steve must have done it in the night. At first, I can't believe Steve would do that, but then I think about it and realise it's exactly the type of thing he'd do. I've always had him pegged as a bit of a psychopath, what with the way he's always manipulating and bullying people to get his own way.

28th June: There's just the two of us left now: me and Steve. Tomorrow, we'll draw lots to see who kills who. I know he's been fixing the draws, using them to control everyone else, and to make sure he not only stays alive, but isn't the one who has to kill anyone. After all, no one gets *that* lucky. I know I haven't been. So far, I've been forced to kill twice. What I don't understand is why Steve has kept me alive so long. Maybe he doesn't see me as a threat because it's clear that, since Jimmy, he's been picking off those most likely to stand up to him. He hides it well, but I swear he's enjoying what he's been making us do.

5th July: I've just finished the last scrap of Steve, and now, if I want to eat again, my only choice is to go outside and face the dead. I didn't wait until the morning to draw lots, because I knew Steve was going to rig it, nor did I sleep the night before we were due to do it, because I didn't trust him. Instead, I sat up, keeping watch and making sure he didn't catch me unawares. It was about four in the morning when I realised I couldn't do this forever, and that I needed to act before he did. That was when I picked up broken chair leg I'd brought down from my office earlier in the day and smashed Steve's head in as he slept. Now I've eaten him, I'm all alone and I realise I'm no better than the dead that are crowding the doors outside. In fact, I may be worse. They do it because they don't know any better, while I knew exactly what I was doing. I keep telling myself I only did what I had to do to survive, but still, there's a part of me that knows it would have been better to die.

8th July: I'm going outside now ...

***

119

Author's Note: *The Custom of the Sea* was a well-established, if rarely spoken of, tradition amongst sailors who found themselves stuck for long periods of time in lifeboats, in the days before modern technology made rescue a real possibility. While the custom said lots should be drawn, the choice of who got killed and eaten first was rarely so democratic, and research suggests lower-ranking men were much more likely to be consumed than their more senior shipmates. If a zombie apocalypse were ever to happen, many people would find themselves trapped in small groups, with little or no access to food. In such circumstances, some will undoubtedly choose to resort to 'the custom of the sea' to stay alive, rather than risk facing the undead.

Winter's End

I saw the first sign of the approaching spring today. I was down in the lower field near the river, looking for animal tracks in last night's snow. It was only a light dusting, but I was confident I'd find some and have a successful hunt for the first time in a week. Instead, I found fresh shoots breaking through the crust of snow which had blanketed the land around us since October. I was never much good with plants, but I think they were snowdrops. We didn't used to get them here, but since my parents stopped farming the fields around here, all sorts of things had moved in.

That was well before the world fell apart, when the first spring plants appeared at the end of January. Now the winters are longer and it's usually March before any dare show themselves. The winters are harsher too, and we struggle to survive, huddled together in a building with ill-fitting boards for windows, and nothing but an open fire to keep us warm. In the past, we'd have snow, but it would only stay for a week at a time, maybe two, before melting away. Now it lies heavily for six months or more, on ground that's as hard as iron. There's no hope of ploughing it, of planting winter crops. All we can do is try to survive off the land and the meagre stores we can build up after the first frosts of autumn start to chill the air.

Mostly we eat meat: rabbits from the warren in the paddock; or roe deer from the wood if I get really lucky. More often, though, it's rats and mice from the barn that once housed chickens. The kids hated eating them at first, but now they're both skilled hunters. They come back with their catch tied by their tails to the stout wooden sticks they use to kill them; showing off and boasting about who's caught the most. Before all this, they'd been disgusted by the sight of whole fish on the fishmonger's slab at the supermarket, but now, they're experts at gutting and skinning their tiny prey before throwing the carcasses into the stew pot.

If there's been a good crop the year before, we'll still have the acorns and beech nuts Mhairi grinds into flour with an old millstone she'd unearthed behind the abandoned cowshed, the first winter we were here. She then turns it into something that loosely resembles bread, and which we can dip into our stew. When the crop's poor, we run out of flour by the winter solstice, and have to resort to eating lichen. It tastes awful but it gives us the vitamins we need to stay healthy, and it stops our stomachs from rumbling.

Before all this happened, I'd been a touch on the heavy side: not exactly fat, but definitely carrying a few extra pounds. Now, I'm all sinew and bone, my muscles wiry, but hardened by the constant exertion needed to stay alive. Once, I went into a neighbouring house looking for any supplies that might have been overlooked by those who'd already ransacked it and was startled to find an old man staring at me out of the gloom, hair limp and straggly, cheeks drawn and gaunt, eyes sunken and bloodshot. At first, I thought he was one them, one of the rotters, and raised my axe, but when the old man did the same I realised he was just my reflection in a grubby mirror that hung on the wall. I'm only forty-one, but the last six years have taken their toll, and I now look closer to seventy.

Still, winter will soon be over and our life will change, as it always does, with the shift from one season to the next. We'll pack the few belongings we still have and leave the remote farmhouse where I grew up. As the snow melts, we'll move up into the mountains. Once there, we'll set up our battered tents in a place where we hope the ground will remain frozen, but where we can still find some food. Up there, there's no chance of rabbits or roe deer, and no rodents to supplement a poor hunt. Instead, we have to rely on catching the small songbirds which hop from rock to rock. They're difficult to trap, and they have little meat on them, but their occasional presence in a diet that consists primarily of lichen and scrubby mountain herbs is a real treat in the lean months of summer.

This is the contrariness of the world we find ourselves trapped in. Winters, while harsh, at least allows us to venture far enough down from the mountains to find shelter in the old farm buildings on the valley floor. There're woods where we can forage, and even a stream we can fish in if we can break through the ice. Then, each spring, the thaw comes, melting the frozen ground, releasing the rotters trapped in its icy grip. Once free, they start their endless search for human flesh. Whenever I dare slip into the valley in summer in search of something more nutritious than we can find in the mountains, I encounter enough to know it's not safe to remain there while the ground's still soft. Once, the first sign of spring was something to celebrate, but now it's a warning that, once again, we'll soon be banished from the lands where I grew up. Each spring we're forced up into the highest reaches of the mountains where the ground remains permanently frozen, and no rotters can reach us before they freeze solid. The chill of winter, the snow, the ice, they're now our friends; the sun, and the heat it gives to the land, our enemy.

I won't tell the others about what I found, not yet. Instead, I'll give them a few more days to enjoy the luxury of being surrounded by four stone walls and all the rats they can catch. I'll let the happiness of winter, when we can move freely without having to worry about the dead, last as long as I can, but I know we'll soon be exiled to the mountains once more.

***

Author's Note: In the grim months at the start of the year, I always long for the arrival of spring and search eagerly for the first signs of the plants coming back to life. What, I wondered, would it be like to live in a world where the first signs of spring were not a welcome sight? What if things were turned upside down, and life was easier in winter than in summer?

This idea then seemed to click with the concept from the novel *World War Z*, that in those regions close to the poles, zombies would freeze solid in winter only to reanimate in spring, when the snow and ice melts away. This gave me the perfect situation in which to set a story where the first green shoots of spring were not a welcome sight, but rather a harbinger of worse to come.

When The Comet Came

'Even those who'd voraciously predicted that the world would end when the comet came were surprised when it actually happened, because it didn't collide with the moon and send it spinning off into space; the Earth didn't shake; the dead didn't rise; there were no tsunamis or volcanoes; and the Christians weren't raised up to heaven. In fact, it took a while for anyone to even realise it was happening.

'It started with the phones. Just as the comet got close enough for everyone to be able to see it, whenever the night's sky was clear enough, the phones went crazy. They'd ring when they shouldn't, and remain silent and lifeless when someone called. They'd suddenly turn off for no reason in the middle of a conversation, or lose reception, even when there was nothing blocking the signal. The phone companies scratched their collective heads, and blamed it on the handset manufacturers. They, in turn, blamed the phone companies right back. There were questions raised in Parliament, but even though it was inconvenient, everyone got used to it after a while. To be honest, it made a nice change to be able to get on a bus or a train without having to listen to three or four half-conversations, all being shouted loudly into separate little black boxes at the same time.

'Then the first plane fell out of the sky — you remember it; the one where the engines stopped working just after take-off from Hong Kong, and it crashed into the sea — that happened the first day the comet outshone the moon. There was a lot of coverage on the news, but nobody realised it was anything unusual until the same thing happened again and again. It wasn't just passenger planes, but cargo and military aircraft too. There was no pattern, no consistency and every conceivable type of plane seemed equally vulnerable. That got people freaked, and pretty much overnight, flying stopped. Business meetings and international conferences didn't happen; Caribbean holidays weren't taken; stag parties had to settle for causing trouble in their home towns; but, on the whole, society carried on as normal. That was until the blackouts started. The comet was visible even in the daytime by then, and the rumour-mongers on the blogs and in the tabloids were putting two and two together, and were ending up with five almost every time. The politicians appealed for calm and told everyone they'd get someone to look into it, but in reality, they knew as much about what was happening as the bloggers.

'As the comet got ever closer, things got ever weirder. People started getting ill without getting better. It wasn't any strange new disease, it was just that the medicines, which had made the pharmaceutical industry so profitable for so long, suddenly stop working. Not just one or two, but pretty much all of them. We'd have gone online and asked the homeopaths and other alternative medicine types what to try instead, but by then, the Internet had been down for a week and the nightly rioting had started.

'Still no one could explain what was going on, even when people started dropping dead in the streets. Again, it wasn't anything new, just your garden variety heart attacks, brain haemorrhages and things like that, but it seemed to be happening a lot more often than before. It wasn't only the old and the infirm either. without antivirals to keep it under control, flu was cutting a swathe through the young and the healthy. It wasn't one strain, it was *all* of them: Spanish flu; swine flu; bird flu; and probably a few others that had never been big enough to get their own tabloid names before. This kept people indoors much of the time; and most only went out to collect their Government food rations, or to go looting. The masks everyone wore to stop themselves getting whatever infections were going around made people bolder, since no one could recognise them, and it was amazing how quickly we all turned into criminals once we realised we could get away with it. Some asked where the police and the army were while all this was going on, but the truth was they were there alongside the rest of us, smashing in the shop windows and breaking into the warehouses.

'The fact that people spent most of their time holed up in their homes meant that when the first block of flats exploded a lot of people died. Maybe it had happened somewhere else before, but how would we know? Both the TV and radio systems had gone down a few days before, and every form of transport which had a microchip in it — and that was pretty much all of them — had ground to a halt, so there was no way to find out what was going on beyond the city limits. There was no one left to give an official explanation, and all we had to go on were the whispers on the street. The more rational said the gas supply must have ruptured; the conspiracy theorists said it was aliens who'd arrived in a spaceship hiding behind the comet. By that stage, I couldn't decide who I believed more.

That day, the comet blazed larger and almost as bright as the sun. It was painful to look at and it meant the old concepts of night and day were pretty much meaningless. If the comet was up when it should have been night there was no darkness; if it was up in the daytime it was like we had two suns that set at different times. There was no longer any rhythm to life and it drove people crazy. That's probably why the random attacks started. Before, the violence had revolved mostly around rioting and looting, meaning it was easy to avoid if you wanted to, but now it could flare up anywhere, at any time, and people started leaving the city. I stuck it out for another week, but then, as the screaming which echoed through the streets grew louder and more frequent, it got too much ... even for me.

'I didn't know where I was going. I just joined the others traipsing along the road out. I've no idea what time it was when I left. or how long I walked for. I'd long since traded my watch for food, not that it worked by then anyway, and with the two-sun effect it was all but impossible to tell what time of day it was. I might have walked for a day, it might have been three. By then. the city was a distant memory. and the flow of people around me had dried up to a trickle. I didn't know where the rest had gone. They just seemed to disappear as we walked. Then I became one of them. Suddenly, realising I had no idea where I was, I sat down at the side of the road to try to get my bearings and found I couldn't get up again. I watched others stagger on as I keeled over and lay amongst the weeds. I rolled onto my back and looked up. The real sun was just setting, but the false sun of the comet still burned high in the sky.

'I tried to work out what had gone wrong, but I couldn't. There wasn't anything new; nothing had really changed. It just seemed like everything that could go wrong had gone wrong at the same time, and we, as a society, couldn't cope. I didn't even know if it had really had anything to do with the comet. That might only have been a coincidence, or maybe it was just the last straw. Maybe we'd pushed the planet too far, and finally, it had pushed back. Or maybe we'd reached a critical mass, and what had happened was inevitable. Maybe our systems were too complex, our machines too complicated, our society too unbalanced between the haves and the have-nots and, unknowingly, we'd been living on borrowed time. The comet's arrival might have just tipped us over the edge of some physical, social or mental precipice we'd been teetering on for years. Whatever the cause, there was no doubt the world I'd once known was gone. I closed my eyes to try to get some rest, but even through my eyelids I could still see the light from the comet.

'I crawled away, looking for shade. Finding a small cave, I pulled myself into the welcoming darkness where I could finally fall asleep. I think that's what saved my life. I didn't leave again for over a week, but I didn't need to. Enough water trickled down the walls that I could quench my thirst by licking it, and I hadn't been troubled by hunger since I'd started walking. I only emerged when I realised it was finally dark outside ... and properly dark at that. I staggered from the cave to find night had fallen, and I frightened myself by letting out a scream of delight. I slumped against a tree and watched the first normal sunrise there'd been in weeks. There was no one else in sight, but a faint smell of rotting flesh drifted towards me on the early morning breeze, from the bodies of people who'd died on the road. I wondered where the comet had gone, but I didn't need to for long. As the sun crossed the horizon I spotted a dark hole on its otherwise glowing disk. Our star, the centre of our solar system, had engulfed the comet and brought normality back to our planet.

'Life will never return to the way it was: too many died, too much was destroyed. But humanity has picked itself up and dusted itself down, and we're slowly putting our society back together again. Before, I didn't really do anything productive, I just worked in a call centre, where I constantly bothered people who really didn't want to speak to me. Someone made a fortune out of it, but it certainly wasn't me or those I called. At the end of each day, I'd spend an hour getting back to a flat the size of a shoebox that I couldn't really afford, but which was worth so much less than I'd paid for it that I couldn't sell it and still be able to pay the bank back. Again, someone was making money out of properties and mortgages, but I was the one drowning in debt. Once home, I'd listen to my neighbours yelling at each other through walls which were too thin, because the construction company put profits before quality. I'd eat lukewarm ready meals that claimed they were made of beef, but tasted like they contained something very different. After that, I'd drink too much beer as I stared at a screen of some kind or other, sometimes two at once, until I passed out. In the morning, I'd get up and do the same all over again. It was existing, but it wasn't really living.

'Now, like almost everyone else who survived, I work the land, and while I still yearn for the old days from time to time, I don't really miss them. I'm not saying life isn't hard, but you have to admit it has more meaning, and in some ways, it's better than it was before. I'm happier knowing that this is all there is. There's no push to always have the newest toys, or the most money, or the hottest clothes; no screens for people to hide behind; and no gossip magazines or paparazzi showing us what some brainless celebrity's been up to, with some footballer who should have been at home with his wife and kids. There's no advertising to make us feel inadequate or unhappy, or tell us what we should be doing, or how we should be looking; to tell us why we can't be content if we don't conform to some ever-shifting norm that someone somewhere has randomly decided is the only way for anyone to live. There are no corporations left to rape the earth for profit, and no banks to tempt you into debt, then trap you there until you end up working as much to pay their shareholders as you do to feed and clothe your family. Social success is no longer judged by the number of friends you have on some arbitrary website, rather by whether any of them will be there for you when you really need them. People talk face-to-face now, like we're doing, rather than simply posting impersonal updates to everyone they've ever met, and quite a few they haven't.

'You can live for today without being told constantly that now is so last year, and that you should really be concentrating on what will be coming next week, or next month, or next year. Yes, that world came to an end, but was it really a world worth saving? We're better off without it, aren't we?'

***

Author's Note: While not a tale of the undead as such, this is still a post-apocalyptic story, so earning its place in this anthology. It was written to mark the fact that, in 2013, two comets would be clearly visible in the night sky above my home. These comets are PAN-STARRS and ISON. In the end, PAN-STARRS put on a pretty good show, and at the current time (November 2013), it looks like ISON might yet live up to its billing as *The Comet of the Century*.

This story is also a critique of modern Western society, particularly its apparent obsession with celebrities, rampant consumerism and the constant bombardment of negativity that is advertising and the media. As the unnamed narrator in the story says at the end: wouldn't we all be better off without it?

The Labyrinth

I stare at the row upon row of metal shipping containers, stacked three high in the car park of the abandoned hospital. From within, comes a cacophony of banging and clattering, letting me know that those inside can sense my presence. When the disease first hit, before anyone knew it did more than kill, the city's morgues had overflowed with the freshly dead. For those in charge, the shipping containers must have seemed like an obvious solution: simply stack the bodies inside, and then cart them away to some anonymous mass grave when the situation finally starts to ease. Only it didn't. Instead, it got unimaginably worse. Not only did ever more people become sick and die, but those who were already dead started to come back to life. Well, you couldn't really call it life. They started to move again; and to attack the living, biting at them, tearing their flesh; consuming them, even though, being dead, they couldn't digest what they swallowed. Instead, their bellies distended, stretching their sallow, waxy skin until it split, spilling their guts across the ground. You would have thought they might have noticed this, but they didn't; they just kept on hunting and attacking and eating, dragging their insides behind them through the dust.

I know I shouldn't be here, that it's too dangerous, but I've no choice. I lean down and gingerly peel back the bandage around my left calf. As I do, the stench of rotting flesh hits my nostrils and I almost throw up. I can't believe something so simple is causing me so much pain. All I did was catch my leg on a rusty nail as I climbed through a gap in an old wooden fence. I wasn't even escaping from the dead, I was just checking out a garden shed to see if it had anything useful in it, which it didn't. At first, I didn't give it a second thought, but within a few hours I could feel the wound start to burn as the infection set in. By morning, the lower half of my leg was red and swollen, and foul-smelling puss had started to ooze from the gash. Initially, I feared I'd somehow caught whatever disease it was that was turning people into the walking dead, but soon I realised it was just your normal, everyday infection. I was so relieved I whooped with joy, then the reality of the situation worked its way into my consciousness: I had what was developing rapidly into a severe infection, and I needed to start treating it right away. I rummaged through my gear, looking for the old first-aid kit I'd picked up in an empty house the previous week. When I finally found it, I was disappointed to find the only thing in it which was anything close to being useful was a bottle of iodine. Being careful not to waste any, I flushed the wound with it every morning and night for the next two days. I hoped it would be enough to sterilise it, but it only seemed to make things worse.

Then I started to smell the characteristic odour of gangrene. It was faint at first, but with each passing day it grew stronger and stronger, until I could barely manage to remove the bandage and sluice out the wound without being sick.

The scent of a gangrenous limb is one of those smells you never really forget, not once you've had your first whiff. Mine was back when I was a medic in the army. I'd entered a house with my platoon leader searching for insurgents, only to find an old man lying on a dirty mattress, his leg missing and the stump wrapped in crude bandages torn from the curtains. I don't know how he lost it, probably an IED or a car bomb, or maybe even one of our shells. Out there in those days, there were countless ways to lose a limb. As the others searched the house, I knelt down beside the old man and slowly removed the makeshift bandage to see if I could help. He didn't flinch, or even move, and I knew why: he was dying. It was just as well there was nothing I could do for him, because the moment the stench of rotting flesh hit me, all I could do was stumble from the house, desperate for fresh air, and throw up for ten minutes straight. By the time I'd got myself together and went back inside, he was dead, but I knew I'd never forget that smell, no matter how long I lived.

When I smelled it again coming from my own leg, I knew I had to do something, or I'd die just like the old man in that house all those years ago. My first thought was to search the local pharmacies, but they'd been cleared of anything useful a long time ago. I double-checked just to make sure, but found nothing stronger than a bottle of paracetamol which had rolled under a shelving unit. I started going further and further afield, hobbling as far as I could each day, but it was the same everywhere. Finally, in absolute desperation, I started to seriously consider going to the hospital.

I'd worked there a few years ago, and I knew where everything was kept. I also figured the threat of the dead that undoubtedly lurked there, waiting for the living, would mean it might not have been cleaned out yet, and there might still be something useful left; maybe some docxycycline, or amoxycillin, or even good old penicillin: any of them would do. After all, you'd have to be mad to even think of going in there: mad, or have absolutely no other options. I put it off for as long as I dared, hoping against hope that my immune system would somehow be able to fight off the infection that was eating through my flesh at an ever-faster rate, but deep down I knew it wouldn't. This morning, when I woke, I realised I had to face up to the reality of the situation I found myself in, and do what had to be done: I'd either have to try the hospital or amputate. And there was no way I was going to survive with only one leg, in a world where the dead walked again, even if I survived doing such an extreme operation on myself.

***

I search the spaces between the containers, wondering how many lie in wait for me there. Maybe they're all safely locked away and there's nothing to worry about. Then again, what if someone had got careless and hadn't closed a door properly on one of containers after they'd put the last body inside? What if some of the containers were so old that the metal had rusted through? What if, in the two months since it all started, the dead inside had managed to buckle the walls and break the welds with their perpetual assaults, freeing themselves from their metal coffins? If any of these, or 100 other possible scenarios which ran through my head, had happened, the labyrinth between the containers would be crawling with them. Once I enter, there'll be no turning back and all I can do is hope that there aren't more than I can handle.

I flinch as I slip the bandage back over my festering wound. It blocks some of the stench, but not all of it, and I can still smell the distinctive odour of my own rotting flesh. Pulling my pistol from my waistband, I remind myself that if I don't get some antibiotics soon I'm going to die anyway. I limp forward, trying to put as little weight on my injured leg as possible. The noise from the dead coming from the containers builds in intensity and ferocity as I draw closer and closer. Slowly, I pass into the shadows between the first of the containers, the banging and moaning echoing all around me, not knowing if I'll live long enough to make it to the other side, but knowing I have no other choice.

***

Author's Note: When trying to survive a zombie apocalypse, while the zombies themselves will represent a major threat they will not be the only danger, and illness and injury are likely to kill many who survive the initial outbreak. In particular, without easy access to antibiotics, even the slightest scratch could prove fatal, just as it did before the discovery of penicillin. This story explores the theme of a person caught up in a horrific situation: they have to choose between dying of an infection; and the possibility of being killed by zombies, while trying to get the medication they need to stop it happening. Life in a zombie apocalypse would be filled with such difficult choices.

Apocalypse Apartments Incorporated

Who'd have thought my biggest problem in coping with the zombie apocalypse would be boredom? I know it's different for others. I can see them struggling and fighting and dying through the telescope mounted in the observatory in the top tower, but there's nothing I can do for them. I'm stuck here in the castle, set high above the nearby town, safely locked away. Yes, there's zombies all around me. Well, I suppose they're not really zombies since they're not dead, but because of the disease they act just like the zombies you see in movies, so that's what I call them. Either way, when they first appeared, all I had to do to keep them out was pull up the drawbridge and I was safe. The thirty-foot-wide moat is more than enough to stop them getting close enough to know I'm here, and even if they could cross it, they'd never get through walls which are six feet thick and made of solid stone.

Unlike those in the settlement below, I don't need to go outside to look for food, or, indeed, any other supplies. There's a well in the main courtyard, and I've got enough stores stashed in what were once the dungeons to last a lifetime. I've got solar panels and a couple of wind turbines, and for those days which are dark and still, I've got a diesel generator and enough fuel to run it day and night for fifty years. When I was bringing all this stuff together, I wasn't worried about zombies or infected, or whatever you want to call them. I simply did it to make enough money to stop the buildings around me crumbling to dust. You see, this had been my family's home for 600 years, and, as an only child, it fell to me to look after it when first my father, then my mother died in quick succession.

At first, I'd hated the fact that the dilapidated and ancient edifice was now my responsibility. At thirty-two, I wanted to be out exploring the world and having fun, not worrying about leaking roofs, rotting timbers and rising damp. Then, one day, as I drove away after yet another disaster which would cost more money than I had to fix, an idea suddenly came to me, and I realised how I could fund not just the repairs, but the complete renovation it had needed for at least a century. It would mean some rather drastic changes, but it would also mean I'd never have to worry about being able to afford its upkeep again. My business plan was simple: I had a building which had some pretty serious fortifications and there were lots of very rich, but very paranoid people out there, who feared civilisation was about to be brought to its knees by some disaster or other that was looming just over the horizon. If you look at it one way, you could say I was selling them insurance against their worst fears; in another, you could say I was ripping them off, because I never believed any of it would actually happen. All I did was build up the supplies and guarantee each of my subscribers a safe, secure and, most importantly, luxurious environment where they could ride out whatever catastrophe they feared was about to turn the world upside down. I converted otherwise unoccupied and unused rooms into upmarket apartments, complete with self-contained plumbing and water filters, and even air-scrubbers. That was just the standard stuff. Depending on each subscriber's personal paranoia, I also offered customisations: stuff like heavy-duty fire power; six-inch thick steel doors; and built-in radiation shields. The only limitation I placed on the subscribers was that, in the event of any crisis, they had to find their own way to the castle. Only once they arrived would my duties begin.

Almost from the moment word started leaking out about what I was offering, I was inundated with requests from the rich and famous, and within the first week, I'd filled every available apartment. That was before I'd even started any of the renovations. By the time I had all the conversion work finished, the apartments were changing hands for almost ten times what I'd originally charged. You'd have thought this would have annoyed me, but it didn't. You see, they weren't buying the apartments, only leasing them, and every time a lease was sold, I got ten per cent of the price. I also had the right to veto any sale if I thought anyone would be too high-maintenance. After all, you've got to be selective if there's a chance you'll end up cooped up with people for months on end, during some disaster or other. Each time an apartment changed hands, the new owner would want to change the decor and the security options, and that had to come through me too. And as you might imagine, my prices weren't cheap.

It was funny, within a matter of six months, owning one of my 'apocalypse apartments', as they were being called by then, had become a status symbol for those who could afford them. That drove demand — and prices — up even further. I started to branch out: buying up other castles, lighthouses, and old military bunkers wherever I could find them, and setting up apartments there too. I even adopted the name everyone was using for them for the company I created to run my little venture, and I officially became *Apocalypse Apartments Incorporated*. That was ten years before everything fell apart, and in that time, while everyone else with ancient family piles was fighting just to keep them from falling down, I was making enough money to keep eight castles afloat, as well as all the other buildings I'd picked up over the years. I'd become an expert in the ultimate home defence, and I was the person everyone turned to when they wanted to do something crazy, just in case their wildest nightmares ever came true.

Then came the zombies, or rather 'the infected'. That was one eventuality I'd never counted on, but luckily it seems my defences are perfect for keeping them out. The moment the first hints that something odd was going on appeared on the news, I expected the subscribers to start turning up, but weirdly, they didn't. No one ever even came near the place. That's one of those little mysteries of the apocalypse I'll probably never find an answer to. I mean, I'd specifically installed a helipad to allow people to get here, even when the roads were overrun but, despite the millions they'd paid to have a safe place to hole up in, in the event of something quite so world-changing actually happening, not one of them ever made it.

This meant I was all alone, totally secure, but all alone. And oh, so bored. In the two years since everything kicked off, I've read every book in the place and I know all the films I have on DVD backwards and forwards. I can repeat the entire script, word for word, without making a mistake, for each and every one of them. I'd tried alcoholism, but I wasn't really built for it: I found being drunk on my own very dull, and hangovers without anyone to commiserate with even duller.

When the world first fell apart, I spent a lot of time in the observatory, keeping an eye out for the subscribers I was sure would be on their way, but once it was clear they weren't going to appear, I stopped hanging out there. It was just too depressing watching all that death and destruction, and people struggling for survival. But after a while, I started going back. I can't remember why, but one day, I found myself walking past the door and thought I'd take a look to see what was out there. I was surprised to find there were still people living amongst the zombies. Well, maybe *living* is stretching it a little. More like eking out a meagre existence, struggling every day to find food, while avoiding being torn apart by the hordes of zombies which haunted the streets around them.

By then, I'd been without human company for so long I found myself drawn into their struggles. I made up names for the survivors, and even some of the more memorable zombies, and I started making up backstories for them. It was like my own little soap opera and I couldn't resist it. It was the first time in months I'd felt alive. I knew I was living vicariously through their struggles, and part of me felt uncomfortable with this, but the rest of me revelled in it. The telescope was so powerful, and the town so far away, I felt detached from them. It was like I was watching some fictional drama unfolding on a television rather than real people living and dying.

You might think of me as callous, but it's not like I didn't try to help. Once I knew they were there, grimly hanging on under the worst imaginable circumstances, I spent weeks and months trying to work out how I could help them, but there's nothing I can do. There's no way I can let them know I'm here, and there's no way I can do anything to help them without risking being overrun, which would pretty much defeat the purpose of the exercise. So, here I am, living in total security, with enough food to keep all the little groups of survivors I watch each day fed for as long as we all live, yet there's no way to get the people and the food in the same place. All I can do is sit here as the zombie apocalypse engulfs the world but passes me by, leaving me with nothing to do but stare through my telescope, bored and lonely, unable to do anything to ease their suffering … or my own.

***

Author's Note: Most zombie stories focus on the struggle for survival, and the trials and tribulations people will face if they are to live rather than die.

However, there is likely to be another side to living through a zombie apocalypse, and this is boredom. This is because, if you managed to find enough food and get yourself somewhere safe, you're basically going to be sitting there twiddling your thumbs much of the time. It's unlikely you'll have many books to read, and there won't be any YouTube to watch cutesy videos of cats doing daft things to while away the hours. Having companions around you might not be much help as it's likely you'll have heard all their stories and jokes within a few days or weeks, and they'll quickly become repetitive. In this respect, living through a zombie apocalypse would be like the old adage familiar to many a soldier: war is long periods of boredom punctuated by moments of sheer terror.

The Black Heart Of The Sea

'It's a strange place this. Never like coming here.' Old John and I were clambering up from where we'd leapt ashore moments before, trying our best not to slip and fall into the waters which churned a few feet below us. He looked up at the lighthouse towering above us. 'Aye, very strange.'

I paused to catch my breath, 'What d'you mean?'

'D'you not notice there's not a scrap of seaweed around here? Anywhere else, the shore would be covered with it, but not here.'

I glanced around. Just as Old John said, the wave-battered rocks to which we clung were clear of the brown algae that fringed every other island I'd ever visited along the west coast of Scotland. 'It could be the sea's just too strong for it to grow here.'

'That's as maybe, but there are no barnacles either, and there ain't no waves strong enough to stop them critters. I tell you, nothing grows on this entire island.' He turned and looked up again. 'And no gulls. Where'd you ever see an island around here without seagulls on it? There's something very wrong when even the shite-hawks won't come near.'

I surveyed our surroundings, and sure enough, there were no grey and white blobs perched on the light or the rocks, and none floated in the skies above the island itself, or over the surrounding seas. For much of our passage here, gulls and kittiwakes had been our constant companions, following in our wake and swooping past the windows as if trying to see in. Yet, they must have deserted us as we made our final approach because, as Old John had just pointed out, there were none here now.

'Come on, lad, no time for dawdling. The sooner we're done, the sooner we can get out of here.'

I turned my attention back to the rocks ahead of me. Old John had already reached the point where they flattened off and the short path up to the lighthouse began. He was standing there, arms crossed, waiting impatiently for me to catch up. From where I stood, he was outlined against the blue sky, his white hair flapping in the wind. He was wearing a yellow oilskin jacket, which had seen better days, and faded cords he kept up with a piece of rope instead of a belt. As far as I knew, there was only one time anyone had seen him dressed differently, and that was when he'd been given his medal for bravery. He'd worn a suit then, but only after much cajoling from all around him. As soon as the ceremony was over, and before anyone could take a photograph to preserve the landmark moment, he'd changed back into his usual outfit.

I scrambled up the last few feet and joined him as he stared out towards the sea, where the ship was now standing off. It would wait there, about a quarter of a mile from the island, until we called on the radio and let them know we'd finished the job we were here to do.

'I always hate this bit.' I shivered as a gust of wind worked its way down the back of my neck. 'I mean, what if something goes wrong and they don't come back for us?'

Old John put his hand on my shoulder and chuckled. 'Lad, they always come back. You think I'd be daft enough to let them set me ashore if I wasn't certain they'd be back for me? Especially in a place like this!'

Without explaining himself further, Old John turned and started up along the path which led to a door set into the base of the lighthouse, and I followed after. Our job was simple: all we needed to do was replace the bulb in the light and then we could leave. There was nothing hard or technical about it; just routine. I'd done it close to 100 times on many different lighthouses, and Old John must had done it thousands since the lighthouses were first converted to electricity, and then automated.

It was on reaching the whitewashed building that I saw the first signs that there was something unusual about this one; the door was gouged and buckled in a manner I'd never seen before. I reached out to trace my finger along one of the deep scars and was surprised to find the door was made of steel. On every other light I'd ever visited, the door was wood and not metal. I shot Old John a questioning glance, but he seemed to know what I was thinking. 'Best not to ask, lad.'

He pulled a large key from his pocket and slipped it into the lock before turning it clockwise and heaving the door inwards. I was surprised by the effort this took. As I followed him in, I examined the door and found it to be almost an inch thick. On the inside, there was not only the keyhole, but also a series of heavy bolts which could be slid into catches on a reinforced frame. This was some heavy duty security, and much more than would be needed to stop the wind getting in. The only explanation I could think of was that it must have been fitted during the war, when people feared a German invasion. There were traces of never-used defences lying half-buried and forgotten all along the beaches of the mainland, and the many islands which lay off its shores.

Old John looked around nervously and then glanced as his watch. 'Right, lad, let's get up there and get this over with. We don't want to be here when the sun goes down; not today, with the full moon on its way.'

Before I could respond, Old John started up the stairs. Left alone, I inspected the circular room. The only light that penetrated the gloom came from the door and that's when it occurred to me; there was something else unusual about this light: it was the only one I'd ever been in which didn't have any windows. I took a step forward and inspected the walls more closely. That's when I realised there had been windows when it was built but for some reason, they'd then been bricked up.

I mulled over why this might have been done as I walked to the foot of the stairs and made my way slowly upwards. By the end of the first spiral the early evening light spilling through the open door had disappeared and I was left feeling my way upwards in the darkness. After what seemed like forever, it started getting lighter again, and I finally found myself in the room below the light. Here, there were windows, but again the door was made of steel rather than wood, and was lined with thick metal bolts.

Suddenly, Old John's head appeared through the trap door in the ceiling. 'What're you waiting for, lad?'

I played with one of the bolts, sliding it back and forth. 'What d'you think all this is about?'

'You never know when you might need them,' Old John answered cryptically. 'Now get up here.'

I climbed up the ladder to find Old John had already taken the light apart and removed the broken bulb. I slipped the pack off my back and took out the replacement. I was always surprised by these bulbs: their light might be visible from twenty miles away, but they looked like overgrown versions of the one I had back home in my desk lamp. I held it out and watched as Old John screwed it into its fitting and then reassembled the lenses around it. These were the true secret to the power of the light. They refracted and concentrated it into a beam that was then directed towards the horizon. As Old John was finishing, I wandered across to the glass and stared out towards the sea. I searched the skies, but as before, there wasn't a single bird in sight: no gulls; no gannets; no kittiwakes; nothing. Next, I turned my attention to the sea itself. That's when I noticed something alarming: there were no ships in sight either; not even our own.

I called out. 'John, the ship's gone.'

Old John didn't stop, or even look up. 'Don't be daft, lad. It can't be.'

I searched the ocean once more just to make sure. 'But it is.'

I heard Old John clamber to his feet and come up behind me. 'Shite! Where'd those buggers get to? You got the radio there?'

I rummaged through my backpack, pulling out the handheld VHF and turning it on before I passed it to Old John.

I watched as he held it to his mouth and pressed the transmit button. 'This is Old John calling *Polaris*. Come in, *Polaris*.' He released the button and we listened intently for a minute before he pressed the button again. 'This is Old John calling MV *Polaris*, come in *Polaris*.' Again we listened, and again there was silence.

'This is Old John calling anyone on this station. Can anyone hear me?'

There was nothing beyond the occasional crackle of static.

Old John's eyes flicked to his watch and on seeing him do this I automatically did the same. It was seven o'clock and it would soon be getting dark.

I scanned the eastern horizon where night was already gathering. 'It looks like we're going to be here for the night.'

'We don't want to be ashore once the sun goes down, not here, not on a full moon and all. I told them this was too much of a risk. Shite! Why didn't I make them listen to me?' Old John paced back and forth for a minute, and then stood staring out towards the sea with his hands interlocked behind his head. 'What the hell are we going to do?'

I glanced around nervously. I couldn't understand why Old John was getting so worked up. He was usually so calm and collected. It wasn't like this was the first time we'd been unexpectedly marooned overnight at a lighthouse, and whenever we were put ashore I always took enough food for a couple of days, for just such an emergency. 'John, what are you worrying about? We'll be fine. Wherever they've gone, they'll be back for us in the morning.'

As he turned to face me, I saw a look in his eyes I'd never seen before: pure terror. 'You know what this place is called, lad?'

I thought for a moment, trying to work out what he was getting at, 'The Black Island Light.'

'No, that's the name the outsiders gave it. You know what the locals call it?' I shook my head. '*An Cridhe Dubh Na Mara* ...'

Coming from the lowlands, I didn't really speak Gaelic, but I'd picked up a smattering of words here and there; mostly from place names. 'I know *Dubh* is black and *Mara* is the sea, so it's the black something of the sea.'

'*Cridhe* means heart, lad. They call it The Black Heart of the Sea.'

'Why's that?'

'They say the waters around this island are cursed. They say nothing can live in them, and that they're so cold nothing rots either. Few of the local fishermen will come anywhere near here. They say there's no point because there's no fish in these waters. Every now and then someone tries, figuring there must be loads of fish around the island because it's never fished, but when they do, most never come back. The few that return are so scared by whatever they found, they never go to sea again.'

Old John's eyes flicked along the horizon, searching for any sign of our ship. 'When there was first talk of a lighthouse being built here, the locals begged the Lighthouse Board not to do it, saying it would be a death sentence for anyone sent to keep it. The Board went ahead anyway, figuring the locals were just worried about losing the regular supply of goods they got from the ships that floundered on the rocks. But right from the start there were problems. There were never any official reports, but very soon, the men were refusing to stay on the island after dark, or to even come ashore on days when the moon was full. And it didn't stop when the light was finished. The first three lighthouse keepers disappeared without trace; so did two of the next three. They found the third locked in the light; his hair turned white from shock. He was dragged before the authorities and accused of murder. He wasn't convicted, but he ended his days in an asylum. Whatever had attacked them had smashed right through the wooden door. That was when they replaced it with the steel one that's there now.

'I don't know what the surviving keeper told those in charge, but from then on, the keepers were under strict instructions to always keep the door locked at night, and to never look outside when the moon was full. They also filled in the windows on the ground floor and all the way up to the room just below the light. While no more keepers disappeared, none stayed more than a few months before requesting a transfer and, unquestioningly, it was always given. That in itself was unusual. None would speak about what happened to them while they were here — not openly at any rate — but rumours got out, as rumours always do. It was said that whenever the moon was full they'd hear what sounded like people outside, attacking the walls and the doors, trying desperately to get in. I know some looked, but those that did refused to tell what they saw.'

'Why?'

'I don't know. Maybe they were scared people would think they were mad and that they, too, would be thrown in the asylum; maybe they didn't think anyone would believe them.'

'But wouldn't they want to try to get to the bottom of what was happening? Try to make sure it didn't happen again?'

'Not everyone's like you, lad. Some like to leave things they don't understand well enough alone. Anyway, the Lighthouse Board was glad when automation came along because it was getting ever more difficult to find people willing to be keepers here. They were down to using drunks and dropouts by the end, and that was even with their official line that lighthouses should always be dry.'

I considered everything Old John had just said, and suddenly I felt a chill run through me. 'What d'you think happens at the full moon?

'I don't know, but I think we're about to find out.' Old John pointed towards the water's edge where something was emerging slowly from the sea.

The sun was just touching the western horizon, while the full moon was doing its best to emerge from the clouds in the east. I stared at the grey creature which was slithering from the water and onto the rocky beach at the opposite end of the small island from where we landed. 'Isn't that just a seal?'

'Not unless seals can walk on their back legs. Look!' Old John pointed further along the beach to where another creature had emerged and was now struggling to its feet. These were just the vanguard and as I glanced around, I could see more, hundreds of them, dragging themselves from the icy waters and onto the rocks and beaches which surrounded us on all sides. I screwed up my eyes as I stared into the gloaming, trying to make out what these creatures were. Then the clouds shifted, allowing the light from the moon to illuminate the land below us; I could see the figures staggering towards the lighthouse clearly for the first time. 'Shit! They're people!'

'They might have been once, but I don't think there's anything human left in them.' Old John sounded scared.

'What d'you mean?'

'Look at them, lad. They're not alive now, are they?'

I turned my attention to the people again and saw what Old Jon meant. While they looked human, their skin wasn't the pink of the living. Instead, it was the waxy grey of the dead.

'But if they're dead ...?' My voice petered out as my brain struggled to understand the events which were unfolding below us. As the dead neared the lighthouse I stared at them with a mix of disbelief and fear. I could see that while they were clothed, most weren't dressed in modern apparel. I could only assume they were wearing the clothes they died in, but if this was true then these were people who'd died over many centuries. I could see sailors dressed like those who'd served under Nelson at Trafalgar, while others were clearly from the Spanish Armada. Then there were those dressed in the clothes of officers from British and German navies, from both the First and Second World Wars. There were fishermen too, some in the thick oilskins of the Victorians, while others wore clothes from more recent times. In amongst these men of the sea were those dressed in the kilts and tartans of the local clans, while here and there were people from older ages: Celts; Picts; even Romans; anyone who'd ever perished in the wretched seas around this god-forsaken lump of rock. Yet, while they were dead, they hadn't rotted; they remained as they were at the moment their last breath had left their bodies; the icy waters which had claimed their lives had also preserved them, keeping their bodies fresh for decades, centuries, millennia.

'Look, lad. There!' Old John was staring off to the left where a figure was staggering forward dressed in the uniform of a lighthouse keeper, not of the present day — automation had made sure this was a vocation that had vanished — but of the past.

'You think that's one of the keepers who disappeared?' I could feel the terror starting to rise up within me.

'Aye, I do. And there's another one. And another.' I followed where Old John was pointing and saw each man still dressed in the clothes he'd been wearing when he died. All that was missing was their caps.

'What d'you think happened to them? How d'you think they ended up ... you know ... dead? I can see how the sailors and fishermen died. I mean they must've been shipwrecked and drowned, but what about the lighthouse keepers? They must have been in here.' That was when it struck me: the heavy metal door; the scratches and dents on it. When the dead crawled onto the land, it was to seek the living. For what, I didn't know, but it seemed like the only thing which could explain all Old John had told me, and all I was now seeing with my own eyes. That's when I realised something. 'Shit, John! We've left the door open!'

Not waiting for Old John to reply, I set off, leaping down the stairs as fast as I dared in the darkness. The nearest of the dead were only yards from the door, and I knew there were only seconds to close it. At the bottom of the stairs moonlight was spilling through the open door, its reinforced surround framing the silhouettes of the approaching dead. I raced across the small circular room and threw my weight against the heavy metal door. It moved, but slowly. A second later, I felt the door shake and then move faster. I glanced round to see Old John had joined me, his face flushed with exertion. He must have seen the panicked look on my face because he turned towards me, 'Don't worry, lad, we'll get it closed in time. There's only a couple more inches to go.'

Just as he spoke a grey hand snaked its way between the door and its frame, followed by an arm. Then another one appeared and another.

Soon there were too many for us to ever hope to get the door closed. Despite its thickness, the door shuddered under the weight of the dead which were growing in number with every passing second.

'What do we do now?' I could hear the panic in my own voice.

'Get back up to the top and get that second steel door closed. It must have been installed in case this ever happened.'

'Will we make it in time?'

'I think so. They don't seem to be able to move very fast.'

I glanced towards the foot of the staircase. 'Are you sure?'

'Lad, after tonight, I'm not sure of anything anymore, but it's our only chance,' There was a brief pause, 'On the count of three. One. Two ...' he took a deep breath. 'Three!'

As one, we leapt across the room and up the first of the stairs. The moment before it passed from sight I heard the metal door swing open and crash against the stone wall. I glanced back and saw a mass of grey-faced figures spill into the room below. At their head were two of the long-lost lighthouse keepers. They moved faster than before, as if spurred on by our presence; the only living things on this bedevilled island of the dead. They disappeared from sight as I ran up the spiral staircase, the sound of my feet on the stone steps echoing off the walls that surrounded us. Below, I could hear the footsteps of the dead following, moving faster with every passing second. I glanced at Old John. I could see his outline ahead of me and I could hear his heavy and laboured breathing. Suddenly, he slipped, crashing hard onto the stairs. I stopped to help him up, but he pushed me away. 'Go on, lad. Get up there and get the door ready. We won't have much time if we're to get it secured before they get there.'

'But ...'

'This is no time for heroics, lad. Just get going.'

I listened for a moment, and could hear the sound of the dead, making no noise other than that of their feet beating against stone. Old John was right. They were closing rapidly and we'd have little time to get the second door shut. I raced ahead and emerged into the room at the top of the lighthouse about a minute later. Once there, I set to work swinging the door shut. It had clearly not been moved in years so the hinges were rusty, but it was lighter than the one at the base of the lighthouse. I managed to get it moving with little trouble, yet I didn't close it completely. Instead, I left just enough space for Old John to slip through before I'd finally slam it shut. No sooner was the door in place than Old John came into view; his face red and dripping with sweat. His lips moved as if he was trying to say something, but he had no breath to spare.

He was just a few steps from the door when, with his legs flagging, he slipped for a second time. He slid backwards down the stairs for a few feet before he managed to stop himself. I started to open the door so I could help. He glanced over his shoulder and then turned to me with a look in his eye that was half-fear and half-resignation. 'Shut the door, lad. Save yourself. I'm done for.'

'But, John ...'

'I said shut the door! Just do as you're told for once. Please!'

Before I could reply, the first of the dead rounded the corner. I stared at him: a bewhiskered Victorian fellow in a black lighthouse keeper's uniform. The waxy greyness of his skin glistened in the light, spilling through the narrow gap between the door and its frame. His eyes were dark, sunken holes, which reflected no light. But while he'd been dead for more than a century, there was no sign of rot or decay, and his flesh remained unblemished. His face was still and no expression distorted his features; no sound came from his mouth. Yet the rest of his body moved; not the fluid movements of the living, but stilted and stiff. I watched as the long-dead keeper reached forward and grabbed Old John's leg. John screamed and squirmed round to face him, kicking out hard with his other foot, but the dead man's grip was firm and ungiving. A moment later, another arrived and grabbed Old John's other leg. Old John, his face contorted with terror, did his best to fight them off, but they were too strong for him. Together, they pulled him down the stairs and out of sight, leaving me alone, listening to Old John's screams and shouts echoing up the stairwell as they carried him away.

My first instinct was to run after them and try to rescue him, but before I could even move, more dead appeared around the corner and my bravery evaporated. I slammed the door shut and slid the bolts home, securing myself within the upper level of the lighthouse. I heard the dead reach the steel door and start attacking it. I heard them as the scratched and tore at the door, causing it to shudder and shake. They clearly knew I was inside and they were desperate to break in. At first, I feared they might succeed, but after a few moments, it became clear the door would hold. Relieved, I rushed up into the light itself. I reached the glass just in time to see Old John emerge from the door at the base of the lighthouse, still fighting as hard as he could, twisting and turning, fear etched onto his face as he yelled and screamed. But there was no hope: six of the dead — two of the long-lost lighthouse keepers, a couple of fishermen in bright yellow oilskins, a naval officer in full dress uniform and a man bedecked in traditional highland dress — had him raised above their heads and were carrying him slowly, but inevitably, towards the sea. I watched helplessly as they reached the shore, but they didn't stop. Instead, they plunged into the sea. A minute later, both the dead and Old John were gone, swallowed up by the waves. The last I saw of him was his head just visible above the surface, struggling to breathe as the waves crashed over his face.

***

For the rest of the night, I sat in the light, knees pulled up to my chest, listening to the sound of the dead as they hammered and clawed at the door, knowing that if the broke in, I'd end up like Old John, being dragged to my death beneath the waves. Yet the people who'd installed the door must have known what they were doing because, despite everything the dead could throw at it, it held firm. It was only as the sun began to reappear over the eastern horizon that the dead finally left. After so many hours of almost constant noise, the sudden silence was unnerving. I pulled myself to my feet and stumbled towards the glass that surrounded me on all sides. From my vantage point high above the island, I watched the dead stagger back to the sea in their ones and twos, shuffle into the water and disappear from sight. I stood there for an hour, watching where the last of them had vanished; waiting to see it they might reappear; wondering if it was finally safe for me to venture outside.

I was brought back to reality by the sound of the radio first crackling with static, and then bursting into life: the ship was calling us. I looked round and found the radio where Old John had set it down the night before. Picking it up, I stared at it as they called again. I glanced round and saw the ship steaming over the horizon towards the lighthouse. At first, I wondered where they'd been. Then, as they called a third time, I wondered how I could ever hope to explain what had happened to Old John to anyone else, when I couldn't even explain it to myself. I lifted the radio up to respond and opened my mouth, but no sound came. I tried again, but still I remained mute. There were no words to convey the horror I had witnessed.

Finally, I understood why no one talked about what happened when the full moon shone on the island the locals called *The Black Heart of the Sea*.

***

Author's Note: The Black Island Light isn't based on a single, real lighthouse, rather it is an amalgam of many I've either sailed past or seen pictures of. The Scottish lighthouses were built and designed primarily by the family of the writer Robert Louis Stevenson, and he drew inspiration for much of his writing from the time he spent working with the family firm, in remote locations around Scotland. Some of these lighthouses are truly amazing feats of engineering that cling to rocks and shoals, which barely reach above the waves. They are built to withstand monster seas and hurricane-force winds, which can blow for weeks on end and swallow whole ships in the blink of an eye. Once home to teams of lighthouse keepers, all of them have now been automated. The lights are operated by the Northern Lighthouse Board and are maintained by dedicated teams, which can only reach them by air (in helicopters) or by sea. While working on the lighthouses, these teams always run the risk of becoming marooned temporarily if the weather takes a sudden turn for the worse. This, together with a strong local folklore filled with strange happenings, makes such a lighthouse the perfect setting for a uniquely Scottish, modern horror story, which mixes the present with the past.

About the Author: Colin M. Drysdale has worked as a marine biologist for almost twenty years. During this time, he has travelled extensively and spent much of his professional career on or near the sea.

He spent six years working in and around the islands of the Abacos in the 1990s, and much of the geography of his debut novel, *For Those In Peril On The Sea*, was based on places he got to know during this time. He is also a keen sailor and has sailed in Scotland, the Bahamas, Florida, Newfoundland and Labrador.

He now lives in Glasgow, where he runs a small business providing mapping advice to ecologists and marine biologists, as well as writing zombie and post-apocalyptic fiction. He is currently working on his second novel; a sequel to *For Those In Peril On The Sea*.

He is a dedicated fan of zombie and post-apocalyptic literature, and regularly posts both short stories and articles on surviving in a post-apocalyptic world on his blog (*cmdrysdale.wordpress.com*).

If you would like find out more about the work of Colin M. Drysdale, visit:

www.ForThoseInPeril.net

www.ingramcontent.com/pod-product-compliance
Lightning Source LLC
Chambersburg PA
CBHW060818120626
46557CB00001B/271